FOOL'S FOLLY

BROTHERHOOD PROTECTORS COLORADO BOOK #9

ELLE JAMES

TWISTED PAGE INC

FOOL'S FOLLY

BROTHERHOOD PROTECTORS COLORADO
BOOK #9

New York Times & *USA Today*
Bestselling Author

ELLE JAMES

Dedicated to my grown children who make me crazy and fill my heart all at once. I love them so very much!

Elle James

AUTHOR'S NOTE

Enjoy other military books by Elle James

Visit ellejames.com for titles and release dates
For hot cowboys, visit her alter ego Myla Jackson at
mylajackson.com
and join Elle James's Newsletter at
https://ellejames.com/contact/

CHAPTER 1

Mattie McIntyre shook her head, lips twitching, as the well-dressed ladies slipped onto the barstools at the counter.

Usually, they never would have parked themselves at the bar, preferring to sit at a table where they could conduct their gossip with a pretense of privacy.

Today was different.

Today, Levi Franks sat at the bar, finishing a cup of coffee and a slice of Mattie's signature apple crumble pie. The man had no idea how he affected the female population of Fool's Gold, Colorado. If he did, he ignored them completely. He rarely spoke to anyone except his friends and coworkers with the Brotherhood Protectors.

Levi slapped a ten-dollar bill on the counter, stood and gave her a nod. "Keep the change."

She gave him a beaming smile. "Thank you, Levi. I hope you have a fabulous day."

His eyes narrowed slightly before he answered, "Uh. Thank you." Then he turned and left the diner to the chagrin of the ladies, who were now committed to the barstools. Mattie fully expected them to move to a table now that the hunk had left the room.

"What can I get you two?" Mattie asked, trying not to smile.

"Coffee," Joyce Whitley answered for both of them.

Mattie cocked an eyebrow at the other woman.

She nodded. "Please."

"Marcy and I are here for coffee before we head out for a day of shopping in the Springs." Joyce Whitley smiled. The wife of Randall Whitley, a prominent insurance salesman and member of the Fool's Gold country club and city council, Joyce was fully engaged as a member of the community, advocating clean streets and park upgrades, sometimes at the expense of the less affluent.

Marcy Tatum, her ever-present sidekick, grinned. "You have the best coffee in town, and I could use a pick-me-up before we head to the city."

The city, Colorado Springs, was only a thirty-to-forty-minute drive through Ute Pass, a commute many made daily to their jobs.

Fool's Gold, nestled in the Colorado Rockies, was popular with tourists and native Coloradans alike. As Colorado Springs continued to grow along with increased traffic and the homeless population, some who could afford to move and didn't mind the travel time to work had migrated out to the quaint little town where Mattie had lived all her life.

Now that she owned her own diner, she'd come to know most of the town's residents, including the two ladies seated before her. She pulled out two clean coffee mugs and set them on the counter.

As was her habit, Joyce sat sideways on her stool, looking out at the street. Her critical eye was always looking for another way to improve the city.

The woman's brow furrowed. "Good Lord, it's Earl Farley," she whispered to Marcy.

Marcy leaned close to Joyce. "I haven't seen him in months."

"Me either." Joyce's nostrils flared as if she smelled something nasty.

Marcy frowned. "I hear he's gone a bit crazy, working that old mine he inherited from his uncle."

Joyce snorted softly. "Looks like he's been *living* in the Fool's Folly, not just mining it."

"Isn't that the mine that's cursed?" Marcy asked.

Joyce nodded. "Randall told me that everyone who has ever owned it has met with a grizzly demise. Earl seems to have escaped that curse so far."

Mattie filled the two women's coffee cups with fresh brew and set a small pitcher of cream between them. She glanced out the window of her diner at the man dressed in tattered, filthy clothes, his face smudged with dirt, his hair matted and greasy.

The man's cheeks were sunken as if he hadn't had a decent meal in way too long.

"Oh, dear," Joyce murmured. "Looks like he's heading this way."

Marcy's nose wrinkled. "I certainly hope not. If he smells as bad as he looks…"

Earl staggered toward the door of Mattie's Diner and tripped over the curb, landing hard on the sidewalk.

"He looks like he's drunk." Joyce dug her hand into her purse.

"What are you doing?" Marcy asked.

"I'm going to call the sheriff and have him hauled off." Joyce unearthed her cell phone and started to punch the three numbers into her phone.

Mattie shook her head. "Don't."

Joyce's finger hovered over the call button. "Don't?"

Mattie rounded the bar and was halfway across the diner, calling out behind her. "I think he's hurt and hungry."

"Mattie, you aren't bringing him into the diner, are you?" Joyce asked. "I mean, look at him."

Mattie ignored Joyce and pushed through the

door. Earl struggled to his hands and knees, blood dripping from a gash in his chin.

Before Mattie reached Earl, Levi Franks appeared beside him and dropped to his haunches. "Sir, are you okay?" he asked, his deep voice gentle as he cupped his hand beneath the man's arm and steadied him.

"I can't seem to get up," he said.

"Is anything broken?" Mattie asked.

"No, no." He shook his head. "I don't think so. It's just that these old bones don't work well lately. Give me a minute."

"I can help you up if you'd like," Levi said.

"I don't want to bother anyone. I just needed something to eat." He glanced up at Mattie. "Miss Mattie has the best meatloaf in town."

Levi smiled up at Mattie. "Yes, she does. Let me help you inside so you can have some of that meatloaf."

"If you don't mind." Earl looked up at Levi.

With Levi on one side and Mattie on the other, they helped the old miner to his feet. He draped an arm over each of their shoulders.

"Better?" Mattie asked once the man was upright, surprised at how light he was and how boney his arms were.

"Always better with a pretty lady around." The old man grinned with the few teeth he had left in his head.

Mattie smiled. "How about we go inside and get some food in you?"

With Levi's assistance, Mattie eased Earl toward the door, pushing through with her hip.

Frowning heavily, the ladies at the counter spun on their barstools, giving Earl, Mattie and Levi their backs.

Mattie nodded toward a booth. "He'll be more comfortable on one of the padded seats."

Carrying most of Earl's weight, Levi angled toward the booth she'd indicated and helped the man settle in the booth.

"Thank you," Earl said. "Most folks would just have left me there. Oh, I would've gotten up soon enough. Just needed to catch my breath."

"Let me get you started with something to drink while I get you a helping of the meatloaf that should be ready about now."

"I'd love a cup of your coffee. It's been a while since I had a decent cup." He looked at Levi. "Let me buy you a cup for helping me."

Levi shook his head. "I just had some."

Earl's brow twisted, and his lips sank into a sad frown. "Oh, well, I guess you're a busy man."

Levi glanced at his watch. "Actually, I have a few minutes." His gaze met Mattie's.

She nodded. "I'll get that coffee." Her heart swelled.

The younger man had recognized the older man's need for company and slid into the seat across from Earl.

She hurried to retrieve the coffee pot and two mugs behind the counter, her heart fluttering at the kindness Levi had shown the weak old man.

Joyce frowned and tapped the rim of her mug. "I could do with a refill," she said, her lips tight and her chin elevated.

Mattie gave her a tight smile. "It'll be a few minutes while I brew a fresh pot." She didn't wait for Joyce's response but left the ladies to return to the booth with Levi and Earl.

If she wasn't mistaken, she heard an unladylike snort behind her.

As far as Mattie was concerned, Joyce could wait until Earl got his coffee and his meatloaf. She didn't look like she'd missed any meals, whereas Earl probably hadn't eaten in a week.

She set the mugs on the table in front of the two men, filled Earl's mug with the steaming brew and started to pour coffee into Levi's.

There was only enough coffee to fill his mug halfway. "I'll be back in a few minutes with a fresh pot."

"This is enough for me. I had two cups with my pie. Any more, and I'll swim out of the diner."

Earl chuckled. "How was that pie?"

"The best," he said. "It's becoming a habit I can't

kick. I'm starting to pack on the pounds." Levi patted his flat belly.

Mattie's lips twisted. The man didn't have an ounce of fat on his big frame. "Earl, I'll be back with your meatloaf plate."

She left the two men, ignored the ladies at the counter and pushed through the swinging door into the kitchen where Deanna Melton, her assistant, was just pulling the meatloaf Mattie had made from the oven.

"Perfect," Mattie said. "Just what I needed." She pulled a large plate from the shelf, sliced a large portion of the meatloaf and laid it on the plate while Deanna scooped a helping of mashed potatoes onto the plate.

"Double that," Mattie ordered. She scooped a heaping ladle full of gravy and poured it over the pile of mashed potatoes, then added a spoonful of sweet peas and three dinner rolls.

Deanna laughed. "Someone's hungry."

Mattie nodded. "Practically passed out on our doorstep, he was so hungry."

Deanna's salt-and-pepper gray eyebrows winged upward. "Who was it?"

"Earl Farley."

Deanna's eyebrows inched higher. "The crazy old miner working the Fool's Folly Mine?"

Mattie pursed her lips. "How do you know he's crazy?"

"Anyone who works the Fool's Folly is crazy." Deanna shook her head. "It's cursed."

Lifting the loaded plate, Mattie turned toward the swinging door. "I don't believe in curses."

"Maybe you don't," Deanna propped her fists on her hips, "but the three previous owners of that mine are proof."

"So, they met an early demise," Mattie said, backing into the door. "It's a coincidence, not a curse."

"I wouldn't want to own that mine for all the gold in Colorado," Deanna said. "I might be getting old, but I have a lot of living left to do before I die of a curse."

Mattie shook her head as she pushed through the door and carried the plate to Earl, the supposed crazy miner working a cursed mine.

Mattie didn't believe in curses, fate or luck. Hard work and good decisions were what led to long and successful lives.

She smiled as she set the plate full of food in front of Earl.

His eyes widened, and he licked his lips, practically salivating.

She held back a chuckle, not wanting to offend the man. "Would you like something besides coffee to drink?"

He cleared his throat. "I got more than I can manage here," he said, his voice husky. Earl's hands shook as he gathered the fork in one hand and the knife in the other.

He loaded the fork with a large piece of meatloaf and the knife with mashed potatoes and peas. Alternating the knife and fork, he tucked into the food with the enthusiasm of a starving man.

"Mr. Farley was telling me about the Fool's Folly Mine," Levi said to Mattie. "Did you know he's the fourth owner of the mine in the past four years?"

Mattie's cheeks heated. Levi hadn't engaged in conversation with her in the weeks he'd been coming in for coffee and pie since he'd arrived in Fool's Gold. She stood still, her tongue momentarily tied. She swallowed hard and reminded herself that he wasn't flirting and that she wasn't a teenager. "I recall hearing something to that extent." Lame. Lame. Lame. Couldn't she have come up with something more interesting to say? Her face burned all the way up to her hair follicles.

"None lasted more than a year." Levi nodded toward the man across from him. "Until Earl."

Earl raised a hand, washed down the bite he'd been chewing with coffee and said, "I've owned it now for thirteen months, since the day my uncle died and left it to me." His brows dipped low. "Some say the mine is cursed. That's a bunch of hooey."

Mattie smiled. "I take it you don't believe it's cursed."

"If it is, I want to be the one to break the curse."

He frowned. "If I don't break the curse, I'm living on borrowed time."

Mattie frowned. "Well, I don't believe in curses, and I hope you live a long and healthy life."

"Thank you, Miss Mattie." Earl smiled up at Mattie. "I tell ya, if this was my last meal, I'd die a happy man. You're a kind woman with a big heart to come to an old man's rescue." Earl nodded toward Levi. "I hope your fella knows how lucky he is to have you."

Again, her cheeks heated. "Oh, Mr. Franks isn't my fella. But thank you for your kind words, Mr. Farley. Now, if you'll excuse me, I've got to get back to my other customers."

"Not your fella?" Earl cocked an eyebrow. "I thought you two were together by the way you both came to help me at the same time." His brow wrinkled. "Hopefully, it's not because you're promised to someone else?"

Mattie shook her head at the same time as Levi shook his.

Earl grinned. "Oh, well then, it can still happen."

Levi's brow dipped. "I wouldn't go that far." He glanced at his watch. "I'm sorry, Mr. Farley, but I'm going to be late for a meeting with my boss if I don't leave now." He pushed to his feet and tossed a twenty on the table. "Make sure you have Miss Mattie pack a meal for you to take with you so you don't go hungry later."

Earl stared at the money on the table. "I can pay for my own meal," he said.

"I'm sure you can, but I'd like to treat you," Levi said with a smile. "Thank you for the good conversation and for allowing me to make a new friend in you." He held out his hand.

Earl took it and shook it firmly. "It's an honor. Thank you for your service. Always had a soft spot in my heart for our men in uniform. Especially those who went the extra mile to serve in the Delta Force."

Levi tipped his head toward Mattie. "Ma'am." For a long moment, he stared down into her eyes, his own narrowing slightly. Then he stepped past her, his shoulder brushing against hers as he left the diner.

In his wake, Mattie's heart pounded, butterflies swarmed in her belly and her shoulder tingled where he'd rubbed against it. For a moment, she felt strangely lightheaded.

"He's a good man, that one," Earl said, his gaze following Levi as the younger man climbed into his truck and drove out of the parking lot. "I swear he's got a hankerin' for you."

Mattie shook herself out of the trance she'd fallen into and smiled at Earl. "I doubt that seriously. We barely know each other, and he doesn't usually say more than two words to me each time he comes in."

"Words don't say everything in a man's heart. Actions, a look, a feeling... Your heart will know."

"You say that like you've been in love before," Mattie said.

Earl nodded, his gaze drifting off to an empty corner of the room. "I may not look like much, but I once fell in love." He smiled sadly. "I made the mistake of letting her get away. I'd give all the gold in Colorado if I could get her back."

Mattie's heart squeezed hard in her chest at the sad look in the man's eyes. "Why can't you?"

"She married another and has since passed away." He reached out and gripped her wrist with surprising strength. "Don't do like me and let love pass you by. When you find it, hold onto it with all your might. Money won't buy you happiness. I know that now. My search for gold led me away from the truth."

"What truth?"

"Love makes a man richer than all the gold in the world." He let go of her wrist and glanced over her shoulder. "Enough of my philosophizing. Your customers want your attention. Thank you again, Miss Mattie."

Mattie left Earl to finish his meal and waited on several customers, including Joyce and Marcy, who were unhappy at being kept waiting for more coffee. They showed their disappointment by walking away without leaving a tip.

Mattie didn't care. She hadn't always owned the diner. In fact, she'd come up through the ranks of being a waitress and living off her tip money. Mattie had learned that the wealthiest patrons weren't always the biggest tippers. Most often, those who could least afford to tip left more money, knowing tips helped supplement the waitress's income. As the morning rush ended, Mattie waved goodbye to Earl as he left with a boxed meal for later that evening. Mattie smiled at the man's renewed energy and happy face.

When she went to clean his table, she found the money Levi had left and something she thought was a napkin wadded into a ball. When she started to throw it into the bin in which she was collecting dishes and trash, something hard and shiny rolled out onto the table.

She stared at it for a moment, unsure what she was looking at. About the diameter of a quarter, it was oddly shaped, like a rock, and it was golden in color.

Her heart skipped several beats as she reached for the stone. No. It couldn't be. Mattie shook her head and pocketed the stone, refusing to get excited about something that couldn't be what it appeared to be.

Still, the stone in her pocket weighed heavily on her mind as she cleaned and prepared the diner for the lunch crowd. Not until mid-afternoon did she have time to look at the rock again.

The more she looked at it, the more concerned she was about carrying it around in her pocket. By three that afternoon, she asked Deanna to cover for her while she ran an errand.

She slipped out of the diner and walked down the street to the jewelry store that carried fine diamonds, silver and gold jewelry. She knew the owner, Thomas Kenner, an older gentleman with years of experience dealing in fine gems and precious metal.

Fortunately, Thomas was alone in his store when she arrived.

Before she could change her mind, she advanced across the floor. "Mr. Kenner, do you have a moment?"

"For you, Mattie, I have all the moments you could possibly need," he said. "What can I do for you?"

She pulled the lump out of her pocket and handed it to the jeweler. "Can you tell me what this is?" As she placed it in his hand, she held her breath and waited for his response.

The man took the rock and placed it under a lighted magnifying glass, his brow furrowing. After barely a moment, he looked up, his eyes wide. "Where did you get this?"

Mattie shook her head. "I...found it." Which wasn't a lie. She'd found it on one of her tables. "What is it?"

"Mattie, dear, it's a gold nugget."

She let go of the breath she'd been holding in a whoosh. Sweet Jesus. "H-how much is it worth?"

He placed it on a miniature scale, noted the weight at nine ounces, keyed numbers into a calculator and looked up. "At the current market rate for gold, it's worth approximately sixteen thousand dollars." His frown deepened. "Where did you find this?"

"Mr. Kenner, I can't say." She held out her hand. "Could I have it back?"

He looked down at the nugget and back up at her, without handing her the gold. "Are you sure you don't want to sell it? You might be able to get even more than sixteen thousand."

She shook her head, her heart racing, her hand still held out.

Mr. Kenner placed the gold nugget in her hand. "You might want to lock that up in a safe until you decide how you want to handle it," he said. "Some folks get a little crazy when they learn about gold nuggets. Like me, they'll want to know where you got it." He stared hard at her. "And they won't back down until you tell them."

A chill rippled from the top of Mattie's spine all the way down her back.

She spun and left the jewelry shop, the gold nugget clutched tightly in her fist.

Sixteen thousand dollars.

She'd been walking around with a nugget worth sixteen thousand dollars in her pocket.

Mattie hurried back to the diner.

Earl had to have left it there. Had he done it on purpose? Or had he laid it down and forgotten it?

Either way, Mattie had to find Earl and give back the gold nugget burning a hole in her hand before anyone else found out she had it.

CHAPTER 2

LEVI COULDN'T STOP THINKING about his encounter with Earl and the pretty owner of the diner in Fool's Gold. Currently between assignments with the Brotherhood Protectors, he'd whiled away the day in the basement at the Lost Valley Ranch Lodge, going through news reports and anything to do with the Fool's Folly Mine, Earl Farley and the prior owners of the mine.

As Earl had indicated in their conversation, the previous three owners had all died less than a year after inheriting the mine.

All had been ruled deaths by accident or natural causes.

Andrew Brown, the first owner to die in the string of deaths, had inherited the mine from his grandfather less than a year before his own demise. He'd been working the mine when he'd fallen and hit his head on a rail track used to transport ore to the surface. The impact had caused bleeding in the brain, and according to the medical examiner, he'd died within an hour while lying there.

His brother, Ross Brown, had inherited the mine from Andrew. He'd been working all day in the mine and had emerged into a rainstorm. While driving home, he'd hydroplaned and skidded off the road. After a state crime lab investigation, no foul play had been detected. The mine owner hadn't been under the influence of any drugs or alcohol. He'd simply been going too fast for road conditions, lost control of the vehicle and careened off the highway and down a steep slope, at the bottom of which were giant boulders. He'd died on impact.

The third mine owner, Earl's Uncle Al Farley, had fallen down a shaft in the mine. He'd been discovered several days later when his girlfriend had tried to contact him with no response. She'd sent the sheriff out to check if he was still working in the mine. He'd found Al's empty truck and no sign of Al. Further investigation, using a mountain search-and-rescue team, finally found him at the bottom of a fifty-foot shaft, having broken his neck in a fall.

As Earl had told Levi in the diner, his uncle had been a superstitious man and had been leery of the whisperings. The man had been very careful entering the mine, no matter which shaft. He'd shored up braces, carried backup lanterns and always watched his back. According to Earl, his uncle wouldn't have just stepped into a mineshaft, and he'd told officials that, pushing them to continue investigating.

Once again, the sheriff's department and the state crime lab had inspected the site. No footprints, signs of struggle or anything else had indicated that Al had been pushed. Therefore, the crime lab had deemed the evidence as inconclusive.

To Levi, three deaths seemed too coincidental.

He worried that Earl would be next in the death toll. After having rescued him from faceplanting on the sidewalk, Levi felt somewhat responsible for the guy. He'd hate for anything nefarious to happen to the man. From what Levi could tell, Earl wouldn't hurt anyone. He just worked his mine and left everyone alone.

"Finding much on the Fool's Folly Mine?" Jake Cogburn, the head of the Brotherhood Protectors Colorado division and his new boss, pulled up a seat beside Levi.

"Yes, but not much. If someone helped these men to their deaths, there were no witnesses." Levi leaned back and stretched his arms over his head, relieving the tension in his shoulders. "The reports I read were county news reports. I'd like to look at the detectives' files to see if they had any persons of interest or questioned any witnesses not reported in the newspaper."

Jake grinned. "We can help you with that. You met

John Griffin. His fiancée, Rachel West, is a sheriff's deputy. She should have access to any files stored at the sheriff's office. I'll put you in contact with her."

"Great." He glanced at his watch. "I should be heading into town. I wanted to look at an apartment building before it gets too late."

Jake leaned back. "You know, there isn't a time limit on how long you can stay here at the lodge."

Levi's lips twisted. "I know, and I appreciate the temporary accommodations."

"I get it," Jake said with a nod. "You need a place of your own. I'm all for you finding that place because it gives me hope that you're committing to the long haul with the Brotherhood Protectors." He laid a hand on his chest. "Pure selfishness on my part. We need good people like you."

Levi stared at the computer monitor. Jake was right. Until yesterday, Levi hadn't committed to staying with the Brotherhood Protectors. Sure, he'd done some short-term security gigs for a day or two at a time, but nothing made him want to go all in.

He missed being on active duty, surrounded by men and women like himself. However, going back wasn't an option. His last injury had earned him a medical review board and a one-way ticket out of the military.

He still walked with a slight limp and ran like a lumbering camel. Not good enough to pass a Delta

Force fitness test. And he'd never be satisfied as a desk jockey in the Army.

Frankly, he didn't fit anywhere. When Hank Patterson and Jake Cogburn had found him drinking beer at a bar outside Fort Bragg, North Carolina, and offered him a job, he'd jumped on it, hoping to find purpose.

Single since he'd lost his wife, he had no one to answer to, tie him down or ground his sorry ass. He was as free as the wind and yet in need of an anchor...roots. When his wife had been alive, he'd had a home wherever she was. After her death, his home had been wherever his team was.

Without his team...he had no home. Leaving active duty had meant leaving his family behind.

Several months of drifting had made him long for connection. The offer to join the Brotherhood Protectors had seemed like the perfect opportunity to team up with people like himself—former military and special forces. Still, he hadn't let himself commit.

Until now.

Meeting Earl and actually talking to Mattie had given him a feeling of finally connecting to this new life.

He gave Jake a tentative smile. "I'm just starting to get my feet on the ground."

Jake nodded. "It takes time. I was so far into my pity party it took Hank Patterson and Joseph Kuntz to pull my head out of my ass and get me back on my feet." He chuckled and looked down at his missing leg. "Foot, in this case. They gave me the best kick in the pants a guy could ever receive."

Levi nodded. He knew Jake had lost a leg in an IED explosion. That fact alone gave Levi hope. If Jake could be successful here on one leg, why not him?

"Knock, knock," a deep male voice called out. "You got company."

Both men looked up.

Gunny Tate led the way down the stairs into the lodge's basement, followed by a pretty red-haired woman.

Levi's pulse quickened, and he straightened to his full height.

As the pretty owner of Mattie's Diner reached the bottom of the stairs, her gaze sought Levi's and held, a slight frown puckering her forehead.

Jake stepped forward with a smile, his hand extended. "Mattie, this is an unexpected pleasure. What can we do for you?"

She shook his hand, her gaze going from Jake back to Levi. "I was hoping Mr. Franks could help me locate Mr. Farley. I went by his house, but he wasn't home, and I'm not exactly sure where his mine is located. I need to speak with him on an urgent matter."

Levi frowned and moved closer. "Is everything all right at the diner?"

Mattie nodded. "He left something on the table I

don't think he intended to leave." She dug into her purse and pulled out something wrapped in a crinkled napkin.

Levi stared down at her hands as she unwrapped the object and held it before them.

"Is that what I think that is?" Jake reached out and took the hard, shiny object from her open palm.

Mattie swallowed hard and bit down on her bottom lip. "If you think it's a gold nugget, then yes. I took it to our local jeweler to confirm. Its approximate value is around sixteen thousand dollars."

Jake whistled. "That's one helluva tip."

"Right?" Mattie shook her head. "He probably set it down and forgot about it."

Jake handed the nugget to Levi. "How can someone forget about something like that?"

Levi turned the nugget over in his hand. "That really is a hell of a tip. What are you going to do with it?"

"I want to return it to Mr. Farley. I'm sure it was a mistake." She stared down at the nugget in Levi's hand. "I imagine he's looking for it now, possibly beside himself, thinking he's lost it. And it might sound weird or paranoid, but I feel like a potential mugging victim, walking around with a rock in my pocket." She laughed. "I need to find Earl and give it back."

"What if it wasn't a mistake, and he left that nugget as a tip?" Jake asked.

"Then I'll deal with it." She sighed. "I just can't carry it around in my pocket forever."

Jake turned to the computer and took a seat at the keyboard. "I'm not as fast at this as someone else we know." He clicked several keys and waited as a face appeared on the monitor.

A man with white-blond hair grinned. "Jake. What's up?"

"We need some computer magic." Jake tipped his head toward Mattie. "Mattie, meet Swede. Swede, this is Mattie, and Levi is here with us, too. They met a miner yesterday who owns the Fool's Folly Mine. Can you give us the location of that mine in less time than it would take me to bumble through the internet?"

Swede nodded. "Sure. Give me a second."

Levi hadn't actually met Swede in person, but he'd been on several video conferences with him, Hank and other members of the Montana branch of Brotherhood Protectors. A former Navy SEAL, Swede was the computer genius behind and in support of the Brotherhood Protectors. If they needed any information, including classified, Swede knew how to get it. They didn't ask questions about how he went about obtaining it.

"Sending you the GPS locations of the mine's entrances, some old drawings of the shafts within the mine and information about how much gold has been removed from it since it was opened."

The man hadn't even been online five minutes.

Levi shook his head. "How does he do that?"

Jake snorted. "If I knew, I wouldn't have to ask Swede to do it for me. Thanks, Swede. Say hello to Hank, Sadie and Allie for me, will you?"

"Roger," Swede said. "Did Hank tell you Allie and I are expecting?"

Jake grinned. "No kidding?"

"I know," Swede shook his head. "Scares the shit out of me. Me? A father?"

"That's great," Jake said. "Do you know what you're having?"

"A boy." Swede shoved a hand through his hair, standing it on end. "Send me in to shoot bad guys or blow shit up. Raising a child? Wow. I don't think I'm ready."

"A baby Swede, huh?" Jake laughed again. "You'll do fine."

"How do you know?" Swede stared at Jake from the monitor, his brow twisted, his eyes deer-in-the-headlights wide.

The big Navy SEAL was scared.

And well he should be.

Most people took childbirth and a state-of-the-art medical system for granted. Giving birth was still dangerous for both mother and child.

As Levi knew all too well.

Sarah, his wife, had died giving birth to their still-born baby girl while Levi had been deployed. He had been on a mission when Sarah had gone to the ER because she'd stopped feeling the baby's movement. Within an hour of arriving at the hospital, both Sarah and the baby had been pronounced dead.

Their baby girl's kidneys had failed to develop correctly. Because her little body couldn't function without them, she'd died in utero.

When Sarah's body had tried to abort the baby, the doctor hadn't been able to stop the bleeding, and she'd died in the operating room.

Yeah, Swede had good reason to be afraid. Raising a child was hard. Getting mother and child through the birthing process was downright terrifying.

Had the baby survived, she would've been ten years old now. She'd be playing soccer, having sleepovers with her girlfriends and her mother would still be alive.

The loss of his wife and baby had left a mark on Levi. He didn't ever want to experience the gut-wrenching grief again that had brought him to his knees and shattered his heart and world into a million pieces.

The only way he could accomplish that was to stay single, always wear protection and refuse to get any more involved than a one-night-stand with no strings. No commitment.

Which didn't explain his need to visit one particular diner every day for coffee and pie.

Levi glanced at the redheaded diner owner.

The pie and coffee were the best he'd ever tasted. If he were truthful with himself, he'd admit it was more than the food and drink drawing him to the diner.

Something about the open, friendly face of the red-haired owner brought him back more often than he should be indulging in the tasty pastry.

Mattie had a natural way of making everyone feel welcome. Her smile and ability to interact with her customers made them feel like she was fully aware of each one of her customers on a personal basis. She listened, responded and got to know the locals and many of the out-of-town guests. She asked about their children, parents and pets, and remembered the names of dogs and high school sports teams.

Levi admired Mattie's ability to connect with people.

Levi didn't feel like he had anything in common with anyone except for people who'd been through the same experiences as he'd endured. Assimilating into civilian society had been more difficult than he'd anticipated.

If everyone was like Mattie, he'd have no problem.

Jake and Swede talked more about other team members before Jake finally hit print on the items Swede had sent.

Levi collected the map coordinates and drawings of the mine shafts.

Mattie held out her hand. "Thank you for finding the mine. I don't want to take up any more of your time."

Levi pulled the pages toward himself. "You can't go out there alone."

Mattie frowned. "I can't ask you to go with me. You have better things to do. Besides, Earl might not even be there."

Still holding the nugget, Levi held it up. "You're right. This gold could give normally law-abiding citizens gold fever. They could attack you and take the nugget away before you could stand your ground."

Mattie blew out a stream of air and fisted her hands on her hips. "I know. I've seen fights break out on Main Street when someone accuses another of jumping a claim or mining horizontally to get to ore beneath another person's property."

"And that's here in a nice town like Fool's Gold," he said, shaking his head.

"That's why I'm nervous about carrying the nugget and visiting the mine. Besides the fact that someone might be motivated to rob me, people say it's cursed. I'm not normally superstitious, but that place's creepy factor is off the charts. Anyone who has been inside it lately claims he can hear whispering in the shafts."

"Do you know how to read a contour map?" Jake asked.

Mattie shook her head. "Afraid not. But I can follow the map function on my cell phone."

"It might not be that simple," Levi warned. "Things look different when hills, valleys and ravines are involved. And if you go inside one of the mine entrances, you'll need someone with you."

"Earl works his mine alone," Mattie pointed out.

"And if he fell down a shaft—" Levi prompted.

Mattie's lips twisted. "If the fall didn't kill him, no one would know he'd fallen until it was too late."

Jake frowned. "I'd go with you, but I have a meeting with a potential recruit in forty-five minutes." He glanced at Levi. "Take Levi. He'll have your back."

Mattie glanced at Levi and sighed. "I didn't mean to drag you into this. I only came here because I thought you might know where to find Earl." She smiled as she gathered the papers. "And you did. Thank you. But I can find him using these. Besides, you probably have more important things to do." Her cheeks flushed a pretty pink.

"Not really," Levi said. "I'm in between assignments."

"Since you're feeling like a walking target with that gold nugget in your pocket," Jake said, "I'll assign Levi as your protector. He'll make sure no one tries to take it from you. He'll also have your back if you venture into the mine. And—" Jake strode to a door, flung it open and reached into a cabinet. He came out with a heavy-duty spotlight. "If you have to go into a mine—which I don't encourage—you'll need a good light." As Jake handed the spotlight to Levi, he frowned. "Seriously, I don't encourage anyone going into a mine around here. Most of them date back to the late 1800s. Safety standards didn't exist back then. You won't know what they used to shore up the shafts or how time and erosion might have affected them."

"I've recently been out four-wheeling along old mining trails," Levi said. "Some entrances are not much more than holes in the side of hills, with boulders strewn around as if they'd fallen from above. I wouldn't trust any of the shafts in those old mines."

Jake nodded. "If you think Earl is hurt inside the Fool's Folly, let us get in touch with the mountain rescue team. They're specially trained to go into mines, caves or canyons to retrieve injured people."

"We can hope he's calling it a day and coming out of the mine," Mattie said. "I can wait to return the nugget until he's out in the open. I'm not keen on entering dark, tight places." She shivered. "I tend to be claustrophobic."

"Traumatic event?" Jake asked.

Mattie nodded. "I was locked in a closet by a bad babysitter who wanted alone time with her boyfriend."

Levi's chest tightened. "I'm sorry you had that happen to you. How old were you at the time?"

"Six." She shrugged and gave her usual cheerful smile. "But that was a long time ago. I learned not to go into dark, tight places if I can help it."

"Did you tell your parents what happened?" Levi asked.

"The babysitter threatened to pull the heads off my dolls if I told. After keeping my parents up all night with night terrors, I broke down and dared to sacrifice my dolls. I told them what had happened. They spoke with the teenager's parents, who assured them that the girl was properly punished and no longer allowed to babysit."

"That was the right thing to do," Jake said.

"We should get going if we want to catch Earl before dark." Levi waved the flashlight toward the staircase leading up to the main floor of the lodge.

He followed Mattie up to the kitchen, through the dining room and out onto the wide porch.

She headed for an older model SUV.

"Let's go in my truck." Levi waved toward his black pickup. "It's four-wheel drive. Some old mining roads aren't much more than washed-out trails."

Mattie turned toward his truck and rounded the front to the passenger side.

He beat her to it, opened the door and waited for her to climb into the cab.

As she passed him, her shoulder brushed against his, sending a shock of electricity racing through him.

He'd always had a soft spot for redheads. But this was different. The surge of desire was instant and incredibly strong.

Once she'd settled into her seat and buckled the seatbelt, Levi quickly closed the door between them. He wasn't in a hurry. He was more afraid that if he'd left the door open much longer, he'd say something incredibly stupid, or worse, pull her from her seat and kiss her soundly in front of everyone.

Levi stepped back and lifted his chin. He couldn't afford to get involved with Mattie. He kept his encounters with women at a minimum to avoid any misunderstandings. He wasn't in the market for a partner, wife or anything else.

His gaze swept over Mattie's lithe form. Beautiful, a blessing to be around, and he had the privilege of escorting her through her tasks. He wouldn't let her down.

He rounded the front of the truck and climbed up into the cab. After one glance at families sitting around on the grass, laughing and eating, how hard could it be to protect one woman?

Well, he was about to find out.

CHAPTER 3

MATTIE SAT BACK in the passenger seat, tongue-tied next to the ruggedly handsome former Delta Force Operative.

What was wrong with her? She spent every day at the diner, talking to people she knew as well as strangers. Why, then, couldn't she converse with Levi like any other customer at her diner?

She shot a sideways glance in his direction and chuckled. Who wouldn't be attracted to the man? His broad shoulders and square chin were amazing. And the way his waist narrowed down to his trim hips and buttocks were a pleasure to ogle as he came and went from her diner. He was always a bright spot in her day, especially since he'd made a habit of coming in every day at the same time.

At the diner, Mattie was always on the move and could put distance between them. Trapped in the cab of his truck for the ride out to the mine left her a little breathless. Her heart pounded, beating so fast her pulse banged against her eardrums.

Focusing on not losing her composure, Mattie studied the man's broad shoulders, taut chest and eyes the color of thick, dark molasses.

Mattie fought the urge to reach across the console and touch his chest. Was it as hard as it appeared?

Her heart kicked up a notch at the thought of resting her fingertips against his naked skin.

And just like that, her entire body heated to an instant inferno.

Thankfully, they had a little way to drive to get to the Fool's Folly Mine, giving her the time she needed to regain her self-control.

Levi eventually left the paved road and drove his big truck along mining trails almost totally reclaimed by the surrounding vegetation.

Just when the trail seemed to disappear, they emerged into a flat, open space with a solid rocky bluff in front of them. In the center of the stone mass was an arched tunnel entrance with slats of wood crisscrossing the opening and a warning sign telling people to STAY OUT – PRIVATE PROPERTY.

"I don't see Earl's truck or motorcycle," Mattie said. "And the trail coming in didn't appear well-worn."

"Then we can scratch this entrance off the list." Levi turned the truck around and headed back toward the highway. Before he'd gone too far, he turned off the faint trail onto another that appeared more traveled. This one had tire marks in the dust and flattened vegetation,

Levi eased the truck along the path, coming to a halt in front of a smaller entrance than the last. Only this one wasn't boarded. It appeared to be a dark opening in the face of the rock wall.

"No truck or motorcycle," Levi said. "Could he have walked up here?"

Mattie shook her head. "The man could barely walk from hunger and exhaustion."

Levi shifted into Park. "Is it worth going into the mine to look for him?"

Mattie shook her head. "If his vehicle isn't here, most likely he isn't here." She leaned back in her seat. "He could've headed to his house while we were at the Lost Valley Ranch."

"On it," Levi swung the truck around and headed back to town.

Mattie crossed her arms over her chest. "I'm going to feel silly if he's back at his house. Rather than bothering you and Jake, I could have waited until he got there."

"You're not bothering me," Levi said. "And you heard Jake. He assigned me to protect you. I'm thankful I have an assignment. I get bored sitting around. And it gives me too much time to think."

"Me, too." Mattie grinned. "Not that I'm bored

often. I do feel sorry for my assistant, holding down the diner while I'm out looking for Earl. She's fully capable in the kitchen. And I have a couple of waitresses coming in to work the evening crowd."

"How long have you had the diner?" Levi asked.

"I'm going on five years," she said. "When I bought it, it hadn't been updated in a decade. I spent a lot of my savings and sweat equity to make it look like it does today."

Levi glanced her way, his eyebrows rising. "You did a lot of the work?"

She nodded. "I had a carpenter work the booths, but I recovered the cushions in the booths and on the chairs. We closed for two weeks while Deanna and I tore out the old tile floors and put in new tiles. Some new appliances, and a fresh coat of paint inside and out, made all the difference."

"I'm impressed," he said.

Her chest swelled. "Thanks. I'm happy with the results, and the business is doing well. I hope to resurface the counters next year and buy a new commercial dishwasher. The one we have still works, but it's old. I'm dreading the day it quits."

Levi turned onto the paved road, heading toward Fool's Gold.

"How long have you lived in Fool's Gold?" Levi asked.

"Most of my life. I left when I got married. We

moved to Vegas. As soon as my divorce was final, I moved back. That's when I bought the diner."

"Why a diner?" Levi asked.

She stared out the window. "Because I can. I spent seven years doing everything I could to make my husband happy. I finally concluded that I could never make him happy. The only person who can make you happy is yourself. My husband blamed everything and everyone else for his unhappiness. He constantly found fault in everything around him, including me. I was never good enough at anything. I wanted to own a restaurant or a diner. He didn't think I could manage it. It would be a money pit."

Levi reached across the console and took her hand. "I'm sorry. He sounds like a complete bastard."

"He wasn't always an asshole to me. But he was always negative and critical of others. I just refused to continue in that negative environment. I had dreams of my own that he refused to acknowledge. We'd drifted apart."

She shrugged. "So, I divorced him. He kept the house. I got cash for my share of the equity in the house, and I moved back to Fool's Gold." She smiled across at him. "Now, you know all there is to know about me. I'm not all that exciting." She smiled. "What about you? Are you married? Have children? Does your family live in Colorado?" She held her breath, waiting for his answers.

For a long moment, he didn't respond.

"I'm sorry," Mattie said softly. "If you don't want to talk about your family, you don't have to."

"It's okay," he said, his lips forming a tight line. "Married once. Not anymore. My folks live in the state of Washington near Tacoma."

She felt like she was prying, but she wanted to know. "I take it that you and your wife didn't have children, or you would've mentioned them."

Levi's hands tightened on the steering wheel. "I had one."

Mattie smiled. "Boy or girl?"

"Girl. Unfortunately, she died in utero, and my wife died from hemorrhaging. They couldn't stop the bleeding or save the baby."

Mattie squeezed her fingers around his. "I'm so sorry."

"It was a long time ago."

"You must have loved her deeply." Mattie sat, quietly shocked and ashamed for the envy she felt for a dead woman who'd also lost her baby. The thought of them made her chest hurt.

As a little girl and young woman, Mattie had always envisioned the man she married as being completely devoted and loving to her.

She snorted softly. Her ex-husband hadn't been devoted or loving. When she'd finally realized she couldn't change him, she'd had to change herself.

Mattie had Levi turn onto a street at the edge of town and drive to the very end.

"Oh good, his truck and motorcycle are here. The truck wasn't here when I first came." Mattie dropped down from the pickup and met Levi at the front of the truck. "Ready?"

He nodded and offered her the crook of his elbow.

She slipped her hand through and held on as he guided her toward the front of the house.

When they reached the house, Mattie could see movement through the windows.

"He's home."

The scent of sulfur surrounded them.

"Something's not right," Levi said, his eyes darting around

Mattie raised the brass door knocker. As she let it fall, she heard Levi yell, "Get back!"

As the metal knocker smacked against its metal base, the house exploded.

Levi threw himself in front of Mattie, knocking her to the ground. He lay over her, covering her body with his, protecting her from the slivers of wood and chunks of debris raining down on them.

"Must...get...up." Mattie struggled to get from beneath Levi. "We have to help Earl."

Levi rolled to his feet and reached down to help her up.

Once she stood straight, her heart sank to her knees. The blast had gutted the house. The roof lay on the ground in front of her.

"He's got to be in there," she whispered. "He could be alive."

"Sweetheart," Levi shook his head, "nothing in that house is alive. But we'll look."

First, Levi called the 911 operator, reporting the explosion and that a man was inside.

Mattie and Levi picked up boards, sheets of plywood, drywall and roof shingles, tossing them into a pile, working the area where Mattie had seen someone walking around inside the house.

Mattie cut her hand on jagged metal several times but kept going.

If Earl was buried in the rubble, he might not have much time before his lungs and chest were crushed.

"I see a hand," Levi announced and dug deeper and faster, tossing debris behind him.

Mattie worked alongside him until they unearthed Earl's head and neck.

Levi reached in and pressed his fingers to the base of Earl's throat, searching for the ceratoid artery.

Mattie held her breath, praying for the old miner.

Levi glanced up with his fingers still on the base of Earl's throat. "I can't find a pulse."

All the air left Mattie's lungs as her heart skipped several beats and then jumped ahead, pushing blood through her veins so hard it echoed throughout her head.

The wail of sirens cut through the pounding pulse

in Mattie's head. She continued to pull away the debris. Tears slipped down her cheeks. Wiping them away, she renewed her efforts until hands clasped her shoulders from behind.

She turned to face Levi.

He shook his head. "He's gone, Mattie."

The tears flowed in earnest now.

Levi pulled her close and wrapped his arms around her. He held her as silent sobs shook her body.

The first responders arrived and surrounded Earl.

Levi guided Mattie to the back of an ambulance, where an emergency medical technician dressed her wounds and gave her a painkiller.

Mattie slipped the pill into her mouth and took the water bottle the EMT handed her. The physical pain would subside, but losing Earl meant she'd failed him. "I should've stayed instead of going to Lost Valley Ranch and then to the mine. He might not have died if I'd been there."

"No, you might have died with him had he invited you into his home." When the EMT was done with Mattie, Levi pulled her back into his arms.

She liked being held in Levi's embrace. His arms were like steel bands, strong and protective.

The fire chief arrived and asked Levi and Mattie questions. Then he went off to perform a preliminary inspection of the destroyed house.

"Are you ready to go?" Levi asked.

Mattie nodded toward the fire chief. "After we talk to the chief. I have one more question."

Levi slipped an arm around her waist and led her to where the fire chief stood with the sheriff.

"Do you know what caused the explosion?" Mattie asked.

The chief nodded. "Damaged gas line. It appeared to rupture, causing a catastrophic explosion. We'll do a more thorough investigation in the daylight, but I'd bet my money on the gas line."

Levi's arm tightened around her waist. "Do you want to go to your place or to the lodge? Jake will want to know what happened before he hears it on the news."

"The lodge," Mattie said. "My ears are still ringing, and whatever they gave me for the pain is kicking in. I feel like I'm drunk or high." She leaned into him as he helped her into his truck and buckled her seatbelt.

Levi climbed into the driver's seat and started the engine. As he pulled away, he turned to Mattie. "Just so you know…like you, I don't believe in curses or coincidences."

Mattie nodded, fresh tears slipping down her cheeks. "I keep trying to think how this could have turned out differently. Had we checked on him earlier, Earl would be with us today."

"You can't second guess your actions. It won't bring him back."

"No, it wouldn't, but it might help us protect the

next owner of the mine from meeting the same end as the previous four."

"True." Levi's eyes narrowed. "Did Earl have any relatives?"

"I don't know. I never saw him with any. He always came in alone." Her heart hurt for the man no one would mourn.

Levi reached for her hand, his big warm fingers wrapping around hers.

She raised it to her cheek, absorbing his warmth and strength.

"My bet is that someone sabotaged that gas line. That wasn't an accident."

Mattie stared at the pile of rubble that had once been Earl's modest home. "I feel sorry for whoever inherits this property. He will be the next target."

CHAPTER 4

Levi drove to the lodge at Lost Valley and parked. Mattie had fallen asleep, her head resting against the passenger window.

When he turned off the engine, she still didn't wake. The painkiller they'd given her must have knocked her out.

He eased out of the driver's seat and rounded the front of the truck to open her door.

Mattie jerked awake and blinked bleary-eyed at the lodge in front of her. "Where…?"

"We're at the lodge. I want to bring Jake and Hank up to date on what happened at Earl's place. Then you can decide if you want to stay here or go back to your place. Either way, I'm staying with you. I think you need someone around in case you're suffering from a concussion."

"I'm all right." She unbuckled her seatbelt and slid

out of her seat. Her foot missed the running board, and her momentum took her to the ground faster than she could react.

Levi's arms came up instinctively, catching her before she collapsed to the hard-packed dirt. "Easy there."

She leaned into him, her body warm against his, igniting a desire he hadn't felt in a while. Her soft curves melted into him, making him long to hold her even closer—skin to skin.

He inhaled her fresh scent, struggling to get a grip on himself as he stood her upright and gripped her arms. "I'll find you a lounge chair or a spare bed. You don't have to sit through my debrief."

"No, no," she said. "I'm fine, just a little groggy from sleep."

Levi gave a short, sharp bark of laughter. "More likely, you're loopy from the pain medication that is kicking your butt."

"Yeah," she said with a smile. "I do feel much better."

"Come on, Loopy. Let's get you settled inside."

Slipping an arm around her waist, Levi led her toward the porch.

The light blinked on, and a few men and women came out onto the porch, spreading out to claim seats.

Jake headed toward them, a frown denting his brow. His fiancée, RJ Tate came with him. "I heard about the explosion at Earl Farley's place." Jake's frown deepened as he stared down into Mattie's face. "I almost jumped in my truck and rushed over to see if you two were caught up in the disaster."

RJ touched Mattie's arm. "Are you okay?"

Mattie nodded. "Just bruised and shaken." She stared into RJ's eyes, her own filling with tears. "Earl didn't make it."

Jake nodded. "We called 911 dispatch and got the word about Earl and that you and Levi were still among the living and not on your way to a hospital." His brow wrinkled. "Did the Fire Chief have an initial theory on what caused the explosion?"

"He did." Levi's jaw hardened. "A damaged gas line caused the explosion. How it was damaged is still to be determined."

"Come up on the porch," RJ insisted. "Gunny is over at the Waterin' hole. Some of us were about to head that way to help out, but we can wait."

"Don't hold up on our account," Mattie said. "I should be heading back to my place. Deanna worked the evening shift at the diner. I have to be up and open for the early morning crowd."

"You can stay the night here," RJ said. "We have empty rooms."

Mattie smiled and shook her head slowly, careful not to jar it and make her head start aching all over again. "I appreciate the offer, but all my things are at my apartment."

"I can fix you up with toiletries and something to sleep in," RJ assured her. "No problem." She held up a hand and smiled crookedly. "I also understand the need to be where you can access your clothes and toiletries. The point is that you have choices. It's up to you."

Mattie looked from RJ to Levi and back. "I still want to go to my place. It's closer to get to work tomorrow morning. I have to be there by four-thirty."

RJ winced. "Ouch. Even I don't get up that early."

Jake snorted. "Yes, you do, when you help Gunny get breakfast for a lodge full of guests."

His fiancée shrugged with a teasing grin. "Okay, so I do. But I don't have to go far to get to work."

"Neither do I," Mattie said. "My apartment is only a block from the diner. I walk most days." She grinned. "I couldn't do that from here."

Levi nodded. "All right. We'll take you home after dinner."

"Sounds good." Mattie's stomach grumbled loudly. She laughed. "Where can we get dinner? I'm sure Deanna is still cooking at the diner."

"Gunny has the grill going at the Waterin' Hole. Why don't you join us for food and a beer?" RJ said.

"I could do that," Mattie said. "Minus the beer. I'm not sure about mixing painkillers and alcohol."

"Not a good idea," Levi said. "Gunny doesn't have meatloaf on the menu, but the sandwiches are good and made fresh. His bacon cheeseburger is good, and so is his turkey club."

"I recommend the shrimp po'boy." A petite woman with dark hair appeared behind RJ. "It's my favorite."

"Hey, JoJo, how are you?" Mattie grinned.

"Great," JoJo said, wiping her wet hands on the sides of her jeans. "I just finished changing the brakes on Gunny's old World War II jeep." She shook her head. "They don't make them like they used to." She clapped her hands together and stared from Mattie to Levi. "I see you're met Levi, one of Jake's newest recruits to the team."

Levi had been around the Lost Valley Ranch long enough to know the machinery around the place wouldn't run as well as it did without the spitfire JoJo. The woman was a magician when it came to all things mechanical.

Max Thornton slipped his arm around JoJo's waist and pulled her back against him. "Glad you got done in time for dinner. I think we're all headed over to get a bite and help Gunny with the evening crowd."

JoJo leaned back and let Max drop a swift kiss on her lips. Their easy displays of affection made Levi's chest tighten. If he wasn't mistaken, he felt strangely envious.

His gaze shifted to Mattie.

After years of distancing himself from relationships, he wondered if he was ready now. If he was, would there be a woman willing to put up with him? Would he be able to open his heart again? Losing his first wife had hurt him so much that he'd sworn never to love again. He hadn't been willing to risk that kind of pain again.

Mattie met his gaze. She reached out a hand and then dropped it, her cheeks flushing pink.

Levi stepped closer and took that hand, holding it down at his side. He didn't want the others to see him holding Mattie's hand as anything other than a friend providing comfort.

He wasn't even sure why he was holding her hand, except it felt right. He sensed that after the explosion, she needed to be grounded. "Come on. We need to eat and get you back to your place for an early night."

The group of men and women meandered down a lighted path leading to the back entrance of Gunny's Waterin' Hole.

They passed through the kitchen, where Gunny smiled and waved briefly before arranging a burger patty onto a bun, topping it with a tomato slice, pickles, onions and three pieces of bacon.

"I'm sold," Levi said. "I'm having the bacon cheeseburger."

Mattie laughed. "It's making my mouth water."

"They're good," JoJo said. "But hold out for the shrimp po'boy."

Mattie nodded. "I will."

"In fact," JoJo said. "Max and I will make it for you."

Max's eyes widened. "We will? I thought I was on bartender duty tonight?"

"I'll serve drinks." RJ pushed through the swinging door into the barroom. "You two take a seat."

"I don't mind helping," Levi said. "I'm getting good at cleaning tables."

RJ shook her head. "You're on duty with Mattie. Besides, I'm sure the explosion impacted you as well." She cocked an eyebrow. "Are your ears still ringing?"

Levi hadn't said anything to Mattie, but he still couldn't hear all that well out of his left ear. "I'm fine," he lied.

RJ's eyes narrowed. "Yeah. Right." She tipped her head toward the barroom. "Find a table. I'll come by to get your drink order."

Levi cupped Mattie's elbow and guided her to a table in the corner nearest the bar.

Mattie frowned. "You aren't fine."

He chuckled as he held her chair. "How do you know?"

She glanced up at him. "You hit the ground as hard as I did and covered me from the flying debris." She pinched the bridge of her nose. "I'm usually good at reading people, except when I'm numb from painkillers. What did the explosion do to you?"

He shrugged. "Like you, a couple of bruises, and I can't quite hear out of one of my ears."

Mattie sank onto the chair, pressing a hand to her left ear. "I know that feeling. It's like I can't quite equalize the pressure on my eardrum."

He nodded. "It'll right itself eventually." He slid onto the chair beside hers and glanced around at the other team members. "I feel like I should be working, not sitting."

"Why?" Mattie glanced around the busy barroom filled with locals and tourists. "Do the Brotherhood Protectors always help out at the Waterin' Hole?"

Levi nodded. "It's one of the conditions Jake insisted on when he and Hank contracted with Gunny to rent a portion of the lodge for the Colorado Division headquarters. When we have downtime between assignments, we help out on the ranch and in the bar." He grinned. "I've helped in the kitchen making sandwiches, and I've mixed a few drinks. But mostly, I clean tables. The work helps Gunny and RJ keep the lodge and bar up and running, and it's good for the team."

Mattie tilted her head. "How so?"

Levi's lips twisted. "It keeps us humble. None of us are too good to serve others. It's what we do. We serve and protect. And we're not above cleaning tables and toilets."

Mattie smiled. "As the owner of Mattie's Diner, I'm the chief financial officer, chef, bottle washer and janitor. It does have a way of keeping you connected and humble. We're all people. We're in this world together. Why not make it a happy place?"

Levi reached across the table and took her hand. "Your customers appreciate your optimism and caring." He squeezed her hand gently. "The pie and coffee are great, but that's not the only reason I come by so often."

Mattie's cheeks flushed a pretty pink. "Really? You never say anything beyond giving me your order."

Suddenly on the spot, he leaned back, releasing her hand. "You and your diner make me feel like I've come home. That means a lot to me. I haven't had a place I could call home for a very long time. I wasn't sure Fool's Gold was going to be it."

"And now?" she asked softly.

He looked out across the room full of people and back to her. "It has potential."

She smiled. "It's been my home all my life. Even after my parents sold the house I grew up in to hit the road and live the retired RV life, I stayed." She grimaced. "Don't get me wrong. I love to travel and see other places, but I always want to come back here. The mountains call to me." She laughed. "Not in a woo-woo kind of way."

He chuckled. "Woo-woo?"

She sighed and touched a hand to her chest. "When I leave, I ache to be back in my mountains. They're a part of me." Mattie laughed. "Have you ever felt that way about any place you've lived? No. Of course not. It's just me." She blushed. "I know. I'm silly, but it's who I am."

"That's not a bad thing. It's part of your charm and why your customers love you." He stared across the table at her, loving that she blushed so easily and that she was passionate about her home.

He'd been passionate about being a part of Delta Force, the missions they'd conducted, and the team he'd been a part of. When he'd lost all that, he'd lost the passion.

Sitting across the table from Mattie, hope took root. He might not have the team and the work he used to be passionate about, but maybe he could reinvent his life and gain a passion for something else. A different career. A different place. A woman who knew who she was, what she wanted and where she wanted to be.

"Okay," JoJo appeared beside them. "I have half a minute. What do you two want to eat and drink?"

"Water and the shrimp po'boy," Mattie responded.

"You won't regret it." JoJo wrote her order on the pad in her hand. "And you?" she asked, turning to Levi.

"Water and a bacon cheeseburger."

"Heart attack on a bun," JoJo said as she wrote down his order. "Got it." She disappeared, leaving Levi and Mattie alone in a room full of people.

Mattie yawned across the table. "I hope I can stay

awake long enough to eat. That pain pill is kicking my ass."

"Hang in there," Levi said. "They don't take long to deliver food to the tables."

As they waited, Mattie entertained Levi by naming the people in the bar with whom she was familiar, giving some family history, what they did for a living and who they'd married or divorced. Several people who passed their table stopped to say something to Mattie, either thanking her for catering an event or raving about her famous apple pie. She addressed them by their names and smiled, genuinely happy to see them.

One man wearing faded overalls and worn, scuffed boots stopped beside their table, his brow furrowed. He pulled his cap from his head before he spoke. "Hi, Miss Mattie," he said, his voice low and quiet.

"Raymond, it's good to see you," Mattie said. "How's your wife?"

"She's getting better. The doc finally figured out what was causing her so much pain. She's getting around better every day."

"I'm glad to hear that. Say hello to Helen for me, and let her know that I miss seeing her at the diner. If you stop by sometime, I'll send a slice of her favorite cheesecake home with you."

The man nodded. "She'd like that." He looked down at the hat in his hands. "I heard you were hurt in that explosion at Earl Farley's place. It had me worried."

She touched his hand. "Thank you for thinking about me. I'm okay, but I'm so sorry about Earl. He was a friend of yours, wasn't he?"

"Long time ago," he said. "Used to get together for a beer here. Until he inherited the Fool's Folly. Gold fever tends to change a man."

"How so?" Mattie asked.

"When I did see him, he talked about hearing whispers and strange noises in the tunnels. He thought he might be going crazy or that the mine was haunted." Raymond looked up, his gaze going from Mattie to Levi and back. "Doesn't make sense to go back in. Couldn't have been worth it when the gold played out back in the early 1900s. He'd have been better off giving the mine to some scholarship foundation and walking away. Anything to avoid the curse." He shook his head. "Now, it's too late."

"Raymond, did Earl have any relatives?" Mattie asked.

The older man snorted. "You mean other than the ones who succumbed to the curse?" His brow furrowed. "His only sister died of breast cancer. Seems to me, he spoke of a niece who lives in the Springs. Kathleen Jones or Smith. I don't remember her last name. I remember Kathleen because it reminded me of a song Helen used to sing." He smiled. "She's a big Elvis fan. That was the only relative Earl ever mentioned. Why do you want to know about Earl's kin?" His eyes widened. "The mine. As his only relative, she'll inherit the mine. You gonna warn her about the curse?"

"Sure. I also wondered who should be informed of Earl's death." Mattie grimaced. "No one wants to be the recipient of the news that her only living relative has died."

"I doubt she'll care. She never made any effort to visit Earl. She probably won't even come to the funeral. Knowing Earl, he probably didn't have any burial insurance. His niece won't be happy if she has to come up with the money for his funeral and burial."

Once again, Levi's chest tightened with sadness for the man who hadn't been much more than a stranger to him. No one would show up for his funeral.

Except for Levi. He would be there for the man he hadn't been able to save.

"I can't stop thinking about Earl," Mattie said as Raymond shuffled past. "I don't know anyone who will come to his funeral. He kept to himself for so long that he lost connection to others, even his good friend Raymond. I can't stand the thought that he'll go out of this world without anyone to celebrate his life or commiserate with his death. I, for one, will be there."

Levi grinned. "I was thinking the same thing. Earl will have at least two people there for his funeral."

Mattie met his gaze and nodded solemnly. "I feel responsible. I know it doesn't make sense, but I feel like there was something I could've done."

"You couldn't have known that gas line was damaged. We're lucky we weren't in the house when it went off."

"And to think, someone might have sabotaged that gas line. If that's the case…he's still out there and willing to kill." Mattie me Levi's gaze. "Who will he target next?"

CHAPTER 5

GUNNY EMERGED FROM THE KITCHEN, carrying a food platter and heading their way. "Who had the heart attack on a bun?" he asked in his booming voice.

Levi lifted his chin. "Guilty."

The retired Marine laid the shrimp po'boy in front of Mattie and the cheeseburger in Levi. "Eat up," he said. "And don't worry; it's on me. From what I heard, you two are lucky to be alive." He shook his head. "Earl…not so much."

"We were just talking about him," Mattie said. "He didn't have many friends. We hate to think no one will show up for his funeral."

"Not that he'd know one way or another, but I get what you're saying," Gunny said. "RJ and I will come. He never had a mean word to say to us or anyone else. It's a darned shame this happened to him."

Mattie's brow puckered. "Yeah. He seemed like a nice man."

Gunny scratched his chin. "Some say he was crazy. I think he was only trying to make a go of that old mine and got obsessed with it. It's too bad he didn't get to enjoy any of the fruits of his labors. As far as anyone else knows, he never found gold." He lowered his voice. "Until yesterday."

"Just makes me wonder," Levi said.

"Whether someone else knew what he'd discovered?" Gunny leaned closer. "The only reason they'd want him dead is if they already knew where he'd found it."

Mattie's eyes narrowed. "And they'd have to be in the line of succession to inherit the mine to claim anything of value within."

"Or, they would have to scare new owners away or kill them to keep from being discovered while they continued mining." Levi lifted his sandwich and took a big bite, chewing on the delicious burger while also chewing on what he'd just said.

Mattie picked up her po'boy. "If Earl's only relative is his niece, she'll inherit the mine." She took a bite of the sandwich and chewed as if she'd just bit into the food version of paradise.

Levi finished chewing his first bite and swallowed. "I would consider the niece a person of interest. Hopefully, the sheriff's office will as well." He looked up at Gunny. "By the way...best burger ever."

Gunny grinned. "We use grass-fed Angus and freshly grown vegetables produced near here."

"The shrimp po'boy is everything JoJo advertised. No regrets here." Mattie took another bite.

Levi dipped a French fry in catsup. "Earl mentioned that a mining speculator had contacted him about selling the mine. He'd told him he wasn't interested."

"Did he mention the speculator's name?" Mattie asked.

Levi shook his head. "No. But how many could there be in this area?"

Mattie laughed. "Probably more than we can shake a stick at.

Gunny snorted. "Damned speculators cheat so many good people out of their homes and property, promising them a return on their investment that never materializes." He glanced across the room to the bar where RJ was waving at him. "Gotta get back to work. You two enjoy and stay away from exploding buildings."

Mattie nodded. "Yes, sir. And thank you for the sandwiches."

"Anytime." He left them and crossed to where RJ was slammed with orders at the bar. Within minutes, he had orders filled and delivered, and then he returned to the kitchen to help there.

"That man doesn't slow down," Levi said.

Mattie nodded, her gaze on the door to the

kitchen. "He's worked so hard to bring Lost Valley Ranch back to life. This place was a disaster when he bought it. He restored it to better than its original glory." She smiled at the bar. "The Waterin' Hole was an addition and a smart move. I'm betting the money he makes here helps supplement when the lodge has shortfalls. The locals love it, and the tourists always find their way here for drinks and sandwiches. Even in the winter."

Levi finished his sandwich and washed it all down with water.

Mattie made it halfway through hers and stalled out. "I'm just too tired to finish. But I don't want to waste it."

"I'll get something to wrap that in." Levi left his seat and entered the kitchen.

Max was flipping burgers on the grill while Gunny assembled lettuce, tomatoes and pickles on buns. "What do you need?"

Having helped out in the kitchen, Levi went straight for the plastic wrap. "Mattie needed some of this to take her sandwich with her."

"We're about to close the grill for the night," Gunny said. "Any last calls?"

Levi shook his head.

"There's supposed to be a meteor shower tonight," Gunny said. "Is Miss Mattie staying?"

"No, sir. She's got to get up early tomorrow to open the diner."

"I can get her to town tomorrow morning," Gunny offered. "I'm up before dawn every day."

"I'll let her know you offered, but I think she'll want to sleep in her own bed." Levi tore off a length of the thin plastic wrap and hurried out of the kitchen and back to the table where he'd left Mattie.

She'd pushed her plate to the middle of the table and laid her head on the table. Mattie was sound asleep, and Levi hated to wake her.

Levi wrapped the shrimp sandwich carefully before touching her shoulder. "Hey. Let's get you home."

Mattie lifted her head and blinked up at him. "Is it already time to go to work?"

Levi chuckled. "No. It is time to get you back home."

She covered her mouth and yawned. "I'm rethinking RJ's offer to stay here tonight."

"Then let's get you into the lodge and settled into bed." He slipped a hand beneath her arm and helped her to her feet.

Mattie swayed and leaned into Levi.

Levi liked how warm and soft she was. His groin tightened. He had to remind himself that she was tired and needed a bed, not a goodnight kiss or anything else. Besides, she hadn't indicated any interest in him other than as someone to lean on.

Once she was steady on her feet, he slipped his arm around her and guided her through the kitchen.

"Heading back to Fool's Gold?" Gunny asked.

"Too tired to go that far," Mattie said. "Is there a couch I can crash on in the lodge?"

Gunny frowned. "Certainly not."

RJ chose that moment to enter the kitchen, carrying a tray full of dirty dishes.

"RJ, show Miss Mattie to one of our empty rooms.

RJ's brows rose. "Decided to stay the night after all?"

"Too tired." Mattie covered her mouth again and yawned. "Are you sure you don't mind?"

"Not at all." RJ set the tray on the counter near the sink, washed her hands, dried them on a towel and turned. "Follow me."

She led the way along the lighted path, up the porch stairs. "If you want to wait here or in the great room, I'll make sure a room is ready and grab some night clothes and toiletries."

"Sounds like too much trouble. Maybe I should go on to my apartment after all."

"Don't be silly. It'll only take me a moment. I can take that sandwich and put it in the fridge, if you like." When she held out her hand, Levi placed the wrapped sandwich in her palm. entered the lodge.

"Gunny said there's supposed to be a meteor shower tonight," Levi said. "Do you want to go in or take our chances and see some of the meteor shower?"

"Meteor shower, as long as we can sit in that porch swing at the same time," Mattie said.

Levi led her to the swing and sat with her, gently pushing his foot against the wooden deck flooring to set the swing in motion.

"It's hard to watch a meteor shower through your eyelids," Mattie said.

"Then don't worry about it as long as you're comfortable.

She leaned her head on his shoulder. "I'm comfortable now." Her body relaxed and melted into his.

He liked it—a lot more than he cared to admit.

Her breathing became deeper.

Levi stared out at the night sky, glad the section of the porch where he sat was engulfed in darkness. He counted four meteors, and the number of breaths Mattie took before RJ returned.

"I have a room ready for you, Mattie." She clapped a hand over her mouth when she noticed Mattie had fallen asleep. "Do you need help getting her up the stairs," she asked.

Levi shook his head. "No, thank you. If you'll lead the way, I'll follow."

RJ strode to the door and waited as Levi scooped Mattie into his arms and carried her across the porch.

RJ opened the door and held it wide as Levi

carried Mattie through. She snuggled into him, her arm draped over his shoulder, her face soft in sleep.

If he turned his head just a little, he could press his lips to hers.

Tucking that thought away, he followed RJ up the stairs to the second floor, turned right and passed several doors before arriving in front of one.

RJ pushed the door open and stood to the side.

As Levi carried Mattie through, she blinked her eyes open and looked around. "I'm not in my apartment, am I?"

He smiled. "No. You're staying the night at the lodge." Levi tipped his head toward the bed. "RJ left a stash of pajamas on the bed, along with toiletries you might need."

"You can put me down now." Mattie cupped his cheek. "Thank you."

He lowered her legs and kept his arm around her until he was certain she could stand on her own.

"I'm good," she said and stepped away. "I'm going to shower and climb beneath the sheets." Mattie stretched and looked around the room and back to Levi. "Where is your room?"

"Down the hall."

She frowned. "Down the hall?

He nodded.

Her lips pressed together in a tight line. "That won't do."

He laughed. "Why not?"

She bit down on her bottom lip. "It's too far."

"Where do you want me to be?" he asked.

She glanced around the room RJ had assigned to her. "Here. I'll even give you the bed and sleep on the chair."

He shook his head. "I'll take the chair. You can have the bed."

"But—" Mattie opened her mouth to argue.

Levi touched a finger to the bottom of her chin and angled it upward. "Irrelevant. Get your shower, and if you feel up to it, we can argue afterward."

She gathered the items, ducked into the adjoining bathroom, set the things on the counter and turned back to the door. "You are staying, right?"

He nodded. "Yes, ma'am."

For a long moment, she hesitated and then disappeared into the bathroom and closed the door. The sound of water running in the shower assured Levi that Mattie could manage on her own.

Levi left her room and hurried to his to jump into the shower, rinse, dry and brush his teeth. After slipping into shorts and a soft T-shirt, he grabbed a throw blanket and hurried back.

He arrived in time to be there when Mattie emerged from the bathroom, wearing an oversized T-shirt that hung down to the middle of her thighs. She'd brushed her hair straight back, letting it fall around her shoulders in damp lengths.

She frowned. "Did you…?"

He grinned. "I did." Settling onto the chair, he tipped his head toward the bed. "Get some sleep. You have to be up early."

Her frown deepened. "You can't sleep like that."

He draped the blanket over his lap. "I've slept in worse conditions. I'll be fine."

Mattie slipped between the sheets and sat in the bed, pulling the comforter up over her. Still sitting, she looked over at Levi. "No. You can't sleep like that. You might as well go to your room and sleep in a real bed."

"I'm not leaving this room unless you kick me out. Do you want me to go?" He cocked an eyebrow.

She didn't answer right away, appearing to think about his question before she sighed and answered. "No. I don't want you to go. But I don't want you to sleep in that chair." Mattie patted the bed beside her. "This bed is big enough for both of us. You can sleep here."

His eyes widened, and his lips twisted. "Uh. No. I don't think so."

Mattie crossed her arms over her chest. "We're both grown adults. We're both wearing more clothes than people wear to the beach. I don't see a problem with sharing a bed to get some sleep."

"You might not." He shook his head. "But I do."

She tipped her head to one side. "Why? Does sleeping with a woman offend your morals in some way?"

"Not at all. It's my lack of morals that concerns me."

Mattie's brow wrinkled. "I don't understand."

He drew in a breath and let it out before explaining. "You really have no idea how tempting you look in that T-shirt, do you?"

She looked down at the soft gray T-shirt. "It's just a shirt."

"And you're just an attractive woman wearing it." He shoved a hand through his damp hair. "When you walked out of the bathroom in that T-shirt, your legs exposed, naked, slender and...well...tempting, it was all I could do not to run from the room to keep from doing something we might both regret. You're a very desirable woman, Mattie."

Her eyes widened. She stared down at the T-shirt and back up. "It's just a T-shirt."

"It's not the shirt." He pushed to his feet, crossed the room and stood in front of her. "It's you." He gripped her arms and stared down into her eyes. "And I've wanted to wrap my arms around you and taste your lips since you walked into this room."

She stared up into his eyes, her tongue sweeping across her lips.

Levi groaned. "You're making this harder than it has to be."

"If you want to leave," she whispered, "go."

He stood still, his hands tightening on her arms. "I don't want to leave. That's the problem."

Her lips quirked upward on the corners. "That isn't a problem for me. Men aren't the only ones who experience desire so strong they can't resist." She cupped his cheeks between her palms, leaned up on her toes and pressed her lips to his. "I've wanted to do that ever since you first walked into the diner."

"I'd never have guessed." His heart pounded against his ribs as he stared at Mattie. It took every ounce of his willpower to keep from crushing her into him. "If I kiss you like I want to, I don't know that I can stop there."

She met his glance with a steady one of her own. "Then don't."

His eyes narrowed. "I haven't committed to a woman since the death of my wife ten years ago."

She cocked an eyebrow. "I'm not asking for strings. I'm a little of a commitment-phobe myself, having escaped an unhappy marriage with a man who thought he could control me by squelching my dreams and desires." She lifted her chin and advanced on him. "I'm not asking for forever." She touched a hand to his chest. "I just want someone to hold me tonight. Tomorrow, we can go our separate ways. No regrets or broken promises."

"Sweet Jesus, woman," Levi muttered. "I should walk away, but I can't."

. . .

MATTIE WASN'T sure what made her throw caution to the wind. Maybe the explosion had shaken everything she knew and made her question her hesitance to commit to a man. Life was short. She had to grab happiness wherever she could, whether it lasted or was as fleeting as a one-night stand.

She was an independent woman, capable of forging her own way in this world alone. She didn't need a man in her life.

But, oh, did she want one.

Not just any man. She wanted...no, desired...this guy.

Levi had proven he was kind and gentle to others. Mattie touched his muscles through his shirt and discovered they were as hard as she'd imagined. She'd rather rip off his shirt and run her hands over his bare skin. "Is it wrong to want you so soon after meeting you?"

He shook his head. "If it is, I'd rather be wrong than right."

"I take it that means you're in for the night?" Mattie shivered in anticipation. She looked up, waiting for his response.

When he nodded, she reached for the hem of his T-shirt, gripped it in her fingers and tugged it over his torso.

Levi raised his arms.

Mattie slid the shirt upward and off his body.

He stood before her, still wearing his jeans and boots, the upper half of his body naked and glorious.

Mattie's hands swept across his skin, imprinting a memory of how his skin felt against her fingertips. She drew a deep breath and let it out slowly with a soft moan.

He chuckled. "You sound like someone having an orgasm over a particularly good piece of chocolate."

She leaned forward, pressed her lips to one of his nipples then flicked it with the tip of her tongue. "Oh, yeah. Only, it's better than chocolate."

Levi snagged the hem of her blouse. "Two can play that game."

Mattie stared up into his face. "I was banking on that." She covered his hands with hers and guided him, dragging the blouse over her head.

He tossed it to a corner and bent to claim her lips in a kiss that stole away her breath.

When he came up for air, they fumbled desperately to remove the remainder of their clothing. Once naked, they fell into the bed, laughing, touching and tasting each other.

Levi laid siege to every inch of Mattie's body, setting her nerve endings on fire and sending molten blood coursing through her veins.

His tongue proved magical when he lowered himself down her torso to the juncture of her thighs.

There he parted her folds and flicked his tongue across her clit.

Mattie gasped, her back arching off the mattress.

"Too much?" he murmured.

"Not…" her breath hitched, "nearly…enough."

He chuckled and bent to taste her again, taking his time to swirl and flick.

Mattie forgot how to breathe, her body tensing as he found and took advantage of that sweet spot that set her world on fire.

She raised her knees and dug her heels into the mattress, urging him to continue.

Levi slid his hand beneath her buttocks and sucked gently on her most sensitive zone.

Mattie flung her head back and moaned, the sensations bombarding her, sending her to the edge of the precipice.

He flicked her once, twice—and bam!

Mattie shot to the heavens, her body pulsing with the force of her release. She dug her hands into his hair and held on, riding the waves all the way to the last.

When she drifted back to the earth and sank into the mattress, she refilled her lungs, her desire only momentarily sated with a longing for more building deep inside.

"Up," she demanded, tugging on his shoulders.

He complied, searing a path with his lips and tongue on the way past her torso to linger at her breasts.

Mattie arched her back, urging him to take more.

He did, sucking one nipple into his mouth where he nipped, flicked and swirled until the tip formed a tight button.

Then he moved to the other breast and gave it the same attention.

By the time he moved up to claim Mattie's mouth, an ache had formed at her core. An ache that could be cured only one way.

She reached for his butt cheeks, gripped them firmly in her hands and guided his cock to her entrance. "I want you," she said. "Inside me. Now."

He shook his head. "Not yet."

Her brow furrowed, and she increased the pressure of her hands on his ass.

Again, he shook his head. "Hold that thought."

Before she could guess his intention, he leaned over the side of the bed, nearly falling off. When he dragged himself back up to the edge, he had his jeans in his hands and dug into his back pocket, retrieving his wallet.

After flipping it open, he dug into the folds and pulled out a foil packet with a triumphant "Ha!" Tossing his jeans to the floor, he tore the packet open with his teeth.

Her patience shot, Mattie snagged the condom, rolled it over the tip of his cock and down to the base, fondling his balls briefly. Then she was back on point, his hips in her grip, his cock poised at her entrance.

"Let's do this," she said, her voice tight, her control tighter, about to be shattered.

"You sure you don't want to be on top? It's easier to call the shots from there." He grinned.

"Shut up and make love to me," she said through gritted teeth.

"Yes, ma'am." His smile slid across his face as he pushed into her.

Already moist from her release and his continued foreplay, Mattie's channel accepted his length and girth easily.

When he paused to allow her to adjust to him, she shook her head. "Don't stop. Bring it fast and hard."

He eased out of her and pressed back in, setting a rhythm she matched by rocking her hips. For each of his thrusts, she rose up to meet him, driving him deeper and harder into her.

He moved faster and faster, driving deeply.

Mattie never felt more complete, more stimulated and more intense than with Levi filling her, stroking her to the core. She rose to the edge for the second time that night and teetered there for a long moment and then shot over the edge.

Levi pressed into her once more, filling her channel with his length and girth, his body tense, his head thrown back. He throbbed inside her, his cock pulsing to the rhythm of her pounding pulse.

When he collapsed on top of her, she didn't care that she couldn't breathe. If she died right then and there, she would die a happy woman, replete and satisfied in every way.

But she didn't die.

Levi rolled to his side, taking her with him.

She dragged in a deep breath and let it out slowly.

"Are you all right?" he asked quietly.

She laughed. "Better than all right." With her head nestled in the crook of Levi's arm, she breathed deeply, letting the tension ease from her muscles.

Back in control of her mind, body and soul, Mattie glanced up into Levi's eyes.

He brushed a strand of her hair back from her forehead. "You were amazing."

A smile spread across her face. "You weren't so bad yourself." She traced a finger over his naked chest and up to his lips.

Levi captured the tip between his teeth and applied a minimal amount of pressure.

"Hey," she said. "That finger's real."

"And it's tasty, just like you." He settled her in the crook of his arm and spooned her body with his. "You should sleep. Four in the morning comes early."

She leaned her cheek against his chest, listening to the sound of his heart beating. "Are you sure you don't want to go for round two?"

"I do. But you have to work. Now, shush and sleep."

Mattie pouted. "I would like to have gone on to the next round."

"We could. But then you'd miss the sleep you need to run a successful diner." He kissed the tip of her nose. "I won't be blamed for your bad mood tomorrow when you're working."

"I'm pretty sure I won't be in a bad mood," Mattie said. "I will likely have to explain why I'm grinning like an idiot all day."

Levi laughed. "Is that a typical morning after for you?"

She shook her head. "Not always. Just so you know, nothing about what we just did felt typical. It was too amazing to be labeled typical. And it's been a long time since my last morning after." She yawned and nestled closer. "Thank you for staying with me. You didn't have to do it."

"I know." He lay for a while without speaking.

Mattie stared at the ceiling, lit by the starlight making its way between the curtains. She closed her eyes but couldn't go right to sleep.

After a while, Levi whispered, "Are you awake?"

She opened her eyes and glanced his way. "No."

"Why?"

She shrugged, liking the feeling of her skin rubbing against his. "I guess you could say I'm basking in the afterglow, and I didn't want to miss a moment of it."

He chuckled.

"Why are you still awake?" she asked.

He didn't answer right away.

When he did, his voice was low and warm, like a caress. "I was thinking."

"About what?" she pressed.

"Commitment."

Her heartbeat stuttered. "What about commitment?"

His hand brushed against her shoulder. "Would the commitment-phobe in you freak out if I call you after tonight?"

Though her heart swelled with joy, she didn't want to sound too thankful and needy. "I don't know," she said, forcing a non-committal tone.

His arm tightened around her. "When will you know?"

She grinned in the darkness, glad he couldn't see her face. "When you call me."

He leaned away from her and reached for his cell phone on the nightstand.

"What are you doing?" she asked.

"Making a call." He held his phone in front of him, his thumb poised over the keys. "What's your number?"

"My number?" She leaned up on her elbow and frowned.

"Your number," he confirmed.

She gave it to him, not exactly sure what he was up to.

He keyed the number into the phone and hit the send button.

Her cell phone jingled on the nightstand. "Seriously? I'm right here." Still, she grabbed her cell phone and answered his call. "Hey."

"Hey." He stared at her in the starlight. "I'm calling. Are you freaking out?"

She grinned. "Strangely, no."

"Me either." He returned her smile. "As one committed to avoiding commitment to another of the same persuasion, I feel we might be on the right track to rehabilitation."

Her lips twitched. "You could be right. What do you propose we do now?"

"Play it by ear, and see where it takes us."

She nodded. "That was vague. I'm a woman who likes an action plan."

"How about this...I take you out to dinner..." he rolled over to look at the clock on the nightstand and turned back, propping himself up on an elbow, "... tonight, and we take it from there."

She nodded. "Or we wait a day or two and see if we still feel the same before we commit to dinner." Mattie cocked an eyebrow.

He stared at her without responding.

"Or not." Her brow dipped. "Do you think we're moving too fast?"

"Absolutely," he answered without pause.

"Then why do you want to go out so soon?"

He pulled her into his arms and kissed her full on the lips. "I like the way you taste, the way you feel in my arms…naked. You'll be at work all day, and I won't get to see you, touch you, feel you." He leaned back. "I think I'll miss you."

She shook her head and answered softly. "Same." Mattie laid her head on his chest. "I'm not gonna lie. It scares me."

"Sweetheart, I'm shaking in my boots."

"Okay. But we take it one baby step at a time." She pressed her hand to his chest. "Agreed?"

He laughed. "I think we leaped way past baby steps here."

"True, but I don't want anyone to get hurt."

He nodded. "No commitment, just dinner."

"Okay."

"Now, go to sleep. I can't have you calling me to say you're too tired to go out with me." He kissed her forehead and lay back on the pillow.

"Goodnight, Levi."

"Goodnight, Mattie."

"And Mattie?" Levi lifted his head.

"Yes?"

"I'm glad you aren't in line to inherit Fool's Folly. I'm beginning to see why everyone says it's cursed."

"Curses don't exist," Mattie said softly.

"Explain that to Earl and the three previous victims."

CHAPTER 6

LEVI FELL ASLEEP SOMETIME AFTER one o'clock in the morning, the last time he glanced at the clock. He must have been more tired than he'd thought. When he woke, the pillow beside him was empty.

He sat up frowning. "Mattie?"

When she didn't answer, he left the bed and padded barefooted to the adjoining bathroom.

She wasn't in there. On further inspection, he noted that the clothes she'd worn the day before were gone, and the T-shirt she'd dressed in after her shower was neatly folded, lying on the nightstand on her side of the bed.

How the hell had she slipped out of the room without him knowing? He must be losing the keen situational awareness that had seen him through many combat scenarios. That wasn't good. If he stayed on with the Brotherhood Protectors in

Colorado, he'd need that keen sense of awareness to keep his clients safe.

He dressed quickly and headed downstairs.

Once on the main level, sounds carried to him, coming from the direction of the kitchen. Levi headed there first, hoping to find Mattie. She'd said she had to be at work early. As he passed through the great room, he glanced at the clock on the mantel. Six thirty. To Mattie, that would be late. She had to get breakfast preparations started earlier than that at the diner. Why hadn't she nudged him awake? He would have taken her into town.

He moved through the great room into the dining room. None of the lodge guests, staff or his team members had gathered yet for breakfast. More than likely, some of them were out tending to the livestock. Gunny would be in the kitchen getting started on breakfast.

Levi pushed through the swinging door into the kitchen and looked around. RJ stood at the gas stove, stirring fluffy yellow scrambled eggs.

JoJo reached into the oven with oven mitts and pulled out a pan full of golden-brown biscuits.

Gunny was nowhere to be seen.

"Good morning," RJ said with a smile. "If you're looking for Gunny, he ran Mattie into town earlier. He should be getting back soon."

Disappointment sat heavily on Levi's chest. He would have liked to hold Mattie close and kiss her again before she left for work. Hell, he would have liked to take her there himself, giving him that much more time with her.

Like they'd both admitted last night, the strength of their feelings toward each other was scary. She'd been in a bad marriage. He'd lost the woman he'd loved. Neither one had been looking for a relationship when they'd stumbled into each other and the potential for something good.

Frightening. More so than facing the business end of the enemy's gun.

"Anything I can do to help with breakfast?" he asked.

"Always," RJ responded. "You could set the tables in the dining room and carry the pitchers of juice and milk out to the buffet."

Levi went to work, hoping to keep busy enough all day to take his mind away from how Mattie's naked body felt beneath him or how perfectly he fit inside her. Or the way her eyes crinkled when she laughed.

Holy hell. He could not be falling for the pretty diner owner so quickly. Love took years to build. He and his wife had known each other since high school. They hadn't married until he was twenty-one, and she was twenty. They'd been together four years before he'd asked her to marry him. They'd been married for three years when she'd died giving birth to their stillborn daughter.

He'd loved her so much and had barely survived her loss, yet time had a way of dulling the pain.

Still, he'd held back, afraid to give his heart away again. He couldn't risk losing someone he loved again.

Then why was he all in on Mattie?

Because she was one badass female, charging through life with grit and determination. He liked that about Mattie. She'd been in a bad marriage with a man who'd attempted to control her. Yet, she now forged her own path and marched to the beat of her own drum.

With her own baggage.

She didn't trust a man to let her be herself. To let her succeed on her own. Yet, she'd proven she could.

Levi recognized in Mattie a woman afraid to open her heart for fear of letting someone take over and call the shots.

Levi knew Mattie could make it on her own. If she wanted to be with a man, it was because of love and desire, not need.

A man would be blessed to have the love of such a woman. And privileged that she would choose him for himself—not because he could rescue her from a dire situation.

His heart swelled at the image of Mattie as a Valkyrie, capable of defending herself, the less fortunate and those she cared most about. Her red hair and fiery passion would arm her with the determination she'd need to conquer any usurper bent on stealing what rightfully belonged to her.

By the time the food was ready, Levi had laid cutlery and napkins on tables throughout the dining room where needed.

Jake and Max came in from feeding the animals in the barn. They washed up and then gathered around the table, talking about the day and the animals.

Gunny entered the dining room, his voice heralding his arrival. "See? This place runs without me." He glanced at the buffet. "Even the food looks better. Are you folks telling me it's time for me to retire?"

"No way," RJ said. "You know how much I hate cooking. "I'd rather shovel horse shit than cook any day."

"Don't worry," Jake said with a short laugh. We saved you some out in the barn."

"Next time, *you* can scramble the eggs," RJ said.

He held up his hands. "Trust me. You don't want that to happen. I haven't met an egg I couldn't burn."

Once the guests had been fed, the staff and the Brotherhood Protectors crowded around the buffet and loaded their plates with food. They settled at the long table.

Levi had to bite down hard on his tongue to keep from asking Gunny if Mattie had made it to the diner all right.

However, the old marine would have told them if there had been any problems.

What Levi really wanted to know was how she was that morning.

Gunny wouldn't have known that answer.

Levi would have to see Mattie in person, standing face to face and listening to what she had to say. Mostly, he'd have to be watching her body language. Levi's strongest instinct was to jump in his truck, drive into town and hit the diner first thing.

As much as he wanted to see her, he knew that would be a mistake. He wasn't one hundred percent convinced he could let down his guard and allow someone into his heart. On the other hand, if he let anyone into his heart, Mattie would be the one. She had more patience, grace and optimism than any woman he'd ever met.

As grizzled and jaded as he'd become. He needed someone like Mattie to soften his rough edges and remind him what it meant to be kind and patient with others. Hell, anyway he looked at it, he needed Mattie more than she needed him.

Maybe he was being selfish, wanting to continue to see her. She could do better than a washed-up Delta Force operator who only knew how to kill things.

"Levi, do you have plans for the day?" Jake asked.

Levi jerked to attention and focused on his boss. "Why? Do you have work for me?"

Jake shook his head. "I'm still waiting to hear from a potential client. I figured you'd want to look into Earl's explosion and the curse of the Fool's Folly Mine."

Levi nodded. "I would like to continue my research."

"Good," Jake said. "If you haven't already, you might want to talk to Swede. He might be able to dig deeper into the backgrounds of the previous owners."

Levi nodded. "I have all the names."

"He can even jump into the criminal databases."

"I'll send the information to him first thing."

Jake touched a finger to his chin, his eyes narrowed. "And you might want to run into Fool's Gold and pay a visit to the sheriff's office and see what they found out by canvassing the neighborhood surrounding Earl's place. Maybe someone saw something."

"I'll do that," Levi said, grateful for any excuse to go to town and possibly stop by the diner to see Mattie before their agreed-upon date night.

After helping clean the dining room, Levi headed down to the Brotherhood Protectors' offices in the basement. He logged onto the computer and brought up the file he'd collected on the Fool's Folly mine and the people who'd owned it.

He stored the information in a sharable file and sent a link to Swede.

Moments later, a video conference call came

through from the Brotherhood Protectors home office in Montana. Levi accepted the call.

Swede's face appeared on the monitor in front of Levi. Even on a monitor, the blond-haired, blue-eyed man appeared larger than life. He could have been a Viking several centuries ago, more comfortable marauding and fighting than poking around on a computer all day.

"I got the link," Swede said without preamble. "I'll get to work on it this morning."

Hank Patterson leaned over Swede's shoulder. "I'm sorry to hear about Earl Farley."

Levi nodded. "So were we."

"I am glad that you and Mattie weren't injured in the explosion," Hank continued.

"Thank you."

"I find it disturbing that the Fool's Folly Mine Curse has taken a turn for the worse and has become more violent." Hank frowned. "Whoever is behind all the attacks and murders has taken it one step further. Subtlety has been dropped completely."

"My thoughts exactly," Levi said. "The next person to inherit the mine could be in grave danger from day one."

Hank nodded. "The sooner we determine who is behind all the attacks, the better." He lifted his chin toward Levi. "Consider this your assignment. I've already notified Jake."

Levi nodded. "Does this mean I'll be protecting

the next person to inherit the Fool's Folly Mine? What if the next person doesn't want a protector?"

"Hopefully, we'll have the murderer caught and the issue resolved before the new owner is notified of his inheritance," Hank said. "He won't have to worry about being targeted. If we're still working on this case after the new owner is identified, we can offer up our services."

Levi cocked an eyebrow. "And if he declines?"

"How would you want to proceed?" Hank asked.

Levi's brow evened. "I feel like I didn't do enough to protect Earl. I'd like to see this through to the end."

"You do realize that some murder cases are never solved," Hank pointed out.

Levi's jaw hardened. "This won't be one of them."

"I urge you to work closely with the Sheriff's Department. We have close ties with them through Griff's fiancée, Rachel West. Keep me informed."

"I will," Levi said.

"And I'll get back to you with anything I uncover," Swede promised.

"We need to get this guy before he gets anyone else," Hank said. "The Fool's Folly Mine owners didn't die because of a curse."

Levi nodded. "Someone's been getting away with murder for far too long."

Hank's lips pressed together in a tight line. "Agreed."

"I'm on it," Levi said.

"Good," Hank smiled. "I only hire the best for the Brotherhood Protectors. Go get 'em."

"Out here," Swede said.

The monitor went dark.

Levi pushed back from the desk, stood and stretched. There had to be more to the story about the Fool's Folly Mine than what appeared on the surface. Maybe there was a disgruntled relative, a claim jumper, a precious metals speculator or a big mining company making a play for the mine.

Someone besides the dead owners had to know something. There had to be a source of information, a person who knew enough about what was going on in and around the town of Fool's Gold to know what was happening with the Fools' Folly Mine located just outside of town.

People like the mayor of Fool's Gold, the sheriff or even the biggest gossip in town. And where was gossip best exchanged? At a local bar or the locals' favorite restaurant.

A place like Mattie's Diner.

If Mattie didn't know, she'd know someone who would. All the more reason to stop at Mattie's diner.

Jake met Levi at the bottom of the basement stairs. "I spoke with Hank. I guess you know already."

Levi nodded. "You wouldn't happen to know who has the pulse of what's going on in Fool's Gold, would you?"

Jake shook his head. "I'm fairly new to this area,

but I tell you who would know. Gunny's a good source of information. And since he owns Gunny's Waterin' Hole, I'm sure he hears a lot of gossip. I'd start with Gunny."

"I will," Levi said. "Then I'm heading into town. Know where I might find Gunny?"

Jake grinned. "He's up in the kitchen. That man can cook."

"Yes, he can." Levi left Jake in the basement and climbed the stairs up to the kitchen.

There he found Gunny up to elbows in dough. The old marine grinned at Levi. "Making fresh bread and pizza dough. It's pizza night at the lodge. Will you be here for dinner?"

Levi shook his head. "Sorry. Got a date."

"With the pretty Miss Mattie?" Gunny asked.

"Yes, sir," Levi said.

"I'm just getting to know you," Gunny said, "and what I've seen so far leads me to believe you're a good guy. Jake wouldn't hire any less."

Levi braced himself. He could feel a "but" coming on.

Gunny punched the dough down and kneaded it a bit longer before continuing. "I've known Miss Mattie for a lot longer. She went to high school with my RJ in Fool's Gold. Miss Mattie smiled more than any girl I've ever met. Then she went off to college, met a boy, married and didn't come back until four years ago. From what RJ said, she went through a heck of a divorce. She gave him everything just to get away from him. That's when Miss Mattie came back home."

Gunny kneaded the dough, putting his muscles into the task.

Levi didn't offer a comment. He wanted to hear more about Mattie and was afraid that if he interrupted Gunny, he'd quit talking about her.

"I don't think I saw that girl smile for the first three months she was back. She wasn't the happy-go-lucky girl from high school. I missed her smile." Gunny gave a sad smile of his own. "She went to work at the diner, worked her way up to manager and then bought the place from the previous owner in just a couple of years. She's come a long way from that girl who came back to Fool's Gold with her tail between her legs. She's smiling again."

"Mattie is pretty amazing."

Gunny pressed hard into the dough. "She's a nice girl and would do anything for anybody. I'd hate to see anyone take advantage of her kind and caring nature again."

Levi drew in a deep breath and let it out slowly. "Message received. I'm glad she's had people like you to look out for her."

"Somebody has to," Gunny said. "She doesn't have anyone else." He grinned at Levi. "I'm sure you didn't come here to watch me knead dough, as fascinating as it can be. Whatcha need?"

"You own a bar," Levi stated.

Gunny laughed. "That I do. What was your first clue."

Levi grinned. "The sign out front. Gunny's Waterin' Hole."

Gunny punched the dough again. "Guilty. I own a bar. And your point?"

"You hear a lot of gossip," Levi said.

Gunny nodded. "More than I want to, at times."

"Have you heard anything in the last five years about any of the owners or relatives of the owners of the Fool's Folly Mine?"

Gunny paused in mid-knead. "Only when one owner passed, and another took his place. Oh, and I heard a bit about Earl's niece in Colorado Springs."

"Were there any other relatives along the way who felt they should have inherited the mine?"

Gunny tilted his head to one side. "At first, yeah. But some of the ones complaining the most eventually inherited the mine after the previous owner died. But let me think about it some more. This old brain isn't the steel trap it used to be. It's more like a sieve, letting memories flow through it like water." He grinned. "Then an hour or two later, that thought or memory will resurface like a buoy popping to the surface."

"While you're thinking about relatives, also think about any mining speculators who might have come through offering to buy the Fool's Folly Mine or any other mine in the area."

Gunny's lips twisted. "There are always mining speculators passing through, offering to buy played-out mines for next to nothing."

"Do you recall any who might have made an offer for the Fool's Folly Mine?"

"Seems to me there might have been one here recently. Too bad you didn't ask Earl before he…"

"True," Levi admitted. "There's a lot of things we should've asked Earl before he died." That tug of guilt pulled at Levi's gut. He should have done more to help the old miner.

Gunny's brow wrinkled. "I know one speculator who usually hangs out at the Coffee Bean in Fool's Gold. I've seen him sitting with the City Manager, Randall Whitley, or the casino manager on several occasions."

"Does he have an office in Fool's Gold?" Levi asked.

"I think he rents a desk at the City Manager's Office in the Fool's Gold Country Club." Gunny grimaced. "I'm not much help, am I?"

"Sure, you are. You gave me a good starting point." Levi rolled his shoulders and cracked his neck. "I'd better get going."

"I hope you find who killed Earl," Gunny said.

Levi nodded. "I'm sure the local law enforcement is on it as well."

"True," Gunny lifted a fat blob of dough, set it in a ceramic bowl and covered it with a dish towel. "I'm sure the sheriff's office is on the case. Earl might have been a bit eccentric, but he was a decent sort. He wouldn't hurt anyone. It's a shame someone hurt him. He didn't deserve to die."

"No," Levi said. "He didn't."

Levi left the lodge and Lost Valley Ranch, heading into Fool's Gold, determined to make headway investigating who blew up Earl Farley's house with the old miner in it and perhaps killed Earl's predecessors.

And if he just happened to stop by the diner, he'd see Mattie. He had questions for her as well—all the more reason to stop by.

He hoped it wouldn't be too soon. Levi hoped she hadn't had second thoughts about last night and their date for later that day.

The only second thought he'd had was that she deserved better than him. Selfish? Yeah. But he didn't want to back out now. Hell, he wanted to see her. The sooner, the better.

CHAPTER 7

MATTIE HAD Gunny drop her off at her apartment that morning, where she'd showered, changed into work clothing and had done her hair and makeup. Then she'd hurried the couple blocks to the diner.

Once there, she'd gotten busy preparing the restaurant for the morning breakfast rush. With Deanna not arriving until just before the lunch rush, it had been up to Mattie to do all the cooking. Her waitresses had handled taking orders and delivering food to the tables.

She'd thrown herself into her work, hoping to fill her mind with her daily challenges, not thoughts of one former Special Forces soldier who'd ripped the rug right out from under her neatly ordered life as a business owner and happily single woman.

She'd been divorced long enough to learn how to live alone and like it. Mattie didn't need a man in her life to make her happy. She was happy just the way she was. No man could improve on that or make her doubt her choice to remain decidedly single.

Then why had every second of the morning been filled with images of Levi? Levi, sitting at the counter every day for the past few weeks... Levi, protecting her from the debris pelting them from the explosion at Earl's place. Levi, making love to her and setting her world and her body on fire.

The more she'd thought about him, the harder she'd worked.

After the morning rush, Mattie carried a trash bag to the large trash bin behind the building. That was when she noticed smoke rising from one of the buildings further down the street. She ran back into the diner and dialed 911.

When the dispatcher answered, she said, "Hi, this is Mattie from the diner. There's smoke coming out of a building a few doors down from the diner to the west."

"We've received calls," the dispatcher said. "The fire department has been notified. Thank you for being a good neighbor."

Mattie ended the call, slipped her cell phone into her back pocket and went back to work, filling orders and cleaning the griddle. She pulled a pan full of biscuits from the oven and popped another in. Several times she ducked out the back door to see if the smoke had stopped billowing from the other building. There was always the danger of one building catching fire and taking out the entire block. She wanted to make sure her customers would get out in plenty of time.

Not long after she called 911, the wail of sirens screamed past her diner on the way to the fire. Mattie checked all the food on the stove and in the oven and then darted out of the kitchen into the dining room to watch as the volunteer fire department raced past her windows.

She stopped Janice, one of her waitresses, and asked, "Did you see where the fire was?"

Janice tipped her head toward one of their customers. "Barnett said it was at the attorney's office down the street."

Mattie frowned. That was a good five buildings from the diner but still on the same side of the street and in the same block of buildings.

"Hopefully, they'll get it under control quickly," Mattie said. "I hope no one was in there when the fire started or that they got out in plenty of time."

"That's Chris Malone's office, right?" Janice asked.

"Yes, it is," Mattie confirmed.

Chris Malone had been the attorney who'd helped her file for divorce and set up her LLC when she'd purchased the diner. He was an older man who'd been in business in Fool's Gold for over thirty years. He'd been talking about retirement for a while. Mattie recalled he'd been playing with the idea of semi-retirement, where he would keep his current clients but not take on new ones and eventually fade out of the market.

Chris had been Mattie's parents' attorney before he'd been hers. He'd helped her through probate when her parents had died in an RV wreck while on their trip around the country, visiting every national park.

Not only was he her attorney, but he was also a friend.

"I hope Chris and his secretary, Linda, are okay." Mattie stared out the window, her heart going out to the man who'd helped her through one of the toughest times of her life.

"Chris and Linda are just fine," Barnett called out. "I saw them standing outside the building when I passed by earlier."

Mattie let go a deep sigh. "Thank God." Knowing they were okay helped Mattie relax and get back to work. She hurried to the kitchen to rescue the food in the pans on the stove and the biscuits in the oven.

After the breakfast rush petered out and before the lunch crowd surged, Mattie took a much-needed break. She grabbed a cup of hot water and a tea bag and carried them to the counter.

Joyce Whitley and Marcy Tatum occupied two of the stools at the bar, their heads bent together as they whispered.

"Good morning, ladies," Mattie said. "Do you

mind if I sit with you? I'm on a brief break before lunch."

Marcy smiled. "Of course not. Please, sit."

Joyce cocked an eyebrow. "Are you sure you should be working? I heard you had a near miss with the explosion at Earl Farley's place."

Mattie nodded. "I'm okay."

"They tell me you were with one of the new recruits from Jake Cogburn's Brotherhood Protectors." Joyce raised a perfectly drawn eyebrow. "What's his name?"

"I was with Levi Franks." Mattie dropped her tea bag into her cup of hot water and braced herself for the interrogation. Joyce was one of the pushiest women in all of Fool's Gold. She didn't let up until she got what she wanted. If she wanted information from Mattie, she wouldn't give up until she had exactly what she desired.

Mattie closed her eyes briefly, too tired to get up and walk away. Resting her feet for a short amount of time was her goal.

Joyce also had a habit of cutting to the chase. "Why were you at Earl's place?"

"We were worried about him," Mattie lied. No matter how much Joyce pushed and badgered, Mattie would not tell her about the gold nugget Earl had left on the table.

"Tommy Kenner said you paid a visit to him yesterday." Joyce tilted her head to one side. "Are you in the market for new jewelry? I can give you the names of the stores I use. Tommy doesn't always carry the quality, clarity and cuts I prefer."

Joyce allowed a long pause, waiting for Mattie to elaborate on her visit to the jewelry store.

Mattie lifted her tea bag out of the hot water and set it on the saucer. She poured a little sugar into her cup and stirred. "It was nice to see Mr. Kenner. I'm afraid I didn't find anything I couldn't live without."

Joyce's eyes narrowed. "He said you hadn't come to shop but to show him something. The dreadful man was quite vague. What in the world did you have to show him?"

Hiding a smile, Mattie lifted her teacup to her lips and sipped before responding. "Did you find something you liked at Mr. Kenner's store?" Nothing like avoiding answering a question by posing one of your own. She smiled at Joyce. "He has a nice selection."

Joyce's brow furrowed.

Marcy stepped in. "Did what you had to show Mr. Kenner have anything to do with Earl?"

Mattie schooled her face to show no emotion. Inside, Marcy's question hit her square in the gut. A man was dead. The entire reason for her visit to Earl Farley's place was to return to him what he'd left on the table in the diner. He'd died before she could complete the task.

Now, she carried that golden nugget in her

pocket, too afraid to leave it lying around in her apartment, car or purse.

Someone had killed Earl Farley.

It had crossed Mattie's mind that whoever killed him might have been after the gold nugget she now carried around with her. If the killer learned that she had it, he might come after her next. All the more reason not to share with these two ladies the nature of her visit to the jeweler, why she'd really gone to see Earl the day before or the fact she carried gold in her pocket. Which reminded her that she needed to go to the bank and put that gold into a safety deposit box.

If she wanted everyone in a fifty-mile radius to know anything, all she'd have to do was tell Joyce Whitley, and everybody who was *anybody* would know within thirty minutes or less.

Mattie was saved from answering Marcy's direct question by the jingle of the bell over the diner door and the entry of the man who'd occupied every waking moment of her day. He stepped through the front door of the diner, his broad shoulders filling the doorway.

Mattie's heart fluttered, and butterflies erupted in her belly. Apparently, she wasn't the only one affected by his ruggedly handsome physique.

Joyce turned on her barstool, a smile curling her lips. "That man could make a woman forget she's married."

Marcy nodded. "Too bad he's only interested in one person."

Joyce's eyes narrowed as she studied Levi and then shifted her gaze to Mattie.

Mattie's cheeks heated under the other woman's scrutiny. Or so she told herself. She wasn't blushing because of the naughty images flashing through her mind of a naked Levi making love to her late into the night before.

Oh, if the ladies beside her could read minds, they would be scorched by the heat in Mattie's thoughts.

Mattie pushed to her feet and rounded the counter. "The usual?" she asked.

He nodded, his gaze on her, and only her. Joyce and Marcy might as well not exist, much to Joyce's well-manicured chagrin.

Mattie snagged a mug from a shelf beneath the counter and filled it with steaming brew from the fresh pot of coffee.

Levi slid onto the stool she'd just vacated and smiled at her.

When he looked at her like that, her pulse pounded, and she found it difficult to catch her breath. "I'll get your pie." She spun and took one step away but stopped when his hand wrapped around her wrist, bringing her to a halt.

"The pie can wait. Can we talk?" He glanced around the diner and tipped his head toward a vacant booth in the corner.

"We can talk." As she passed Joyce and Marcy, Mattie ignored their raised eyebrows and smirks. She didn't give a damn what they thought. Not when Levi hadn't waited until their date night to see her.

Her pulse beating a rapid tattoo, she led the way to the booth in the corner and sat with her back to the ladies at the counter.

Levi took the seat across from her, his back to the exterior wall. He smiled across the table. "How are you?"

She almost laughed at the mundane question she wanted to answer with *fine, crazy, obsessed, thinking of you all day long, couldn't focus on anything else.*

Why were her thoughts so...chaotic? He was just a man.

A handsome man with dark hair with some gray showing at his temples. And those brown-black eyes directed at her seemed to melt the bones in her knees.

She was divorced and happily single, she reminded herself.

But when he reached across the table for her hand, she happily placed hers in his and reveled in how warm and strong his fingers were when he wrapped them around hers.

"I'm glad you made it to work on time. I would've taken you had you woken me. Next time, I'll set an alarm."

Her heart flipped at those two words.

Next time.

Since she'd left their bed that morning, she wondered if what they'd experienced the night before had been a fluke—a one-and-done night of sex. Would Levi have second thoughts about seeing her again?

The fact that he was sitting across the table from her, holding her hand, seemed to be a good indication he wasn't having second thoughts.

Mattie, on the other hand, had been second-guessing herself all morning. The man had been married to a woman he'd loved and had lost her in childbirth along with the child she'd been carrying.

How could she compete with a dead woman?

And did she want to compete?

One lousy marriage had made Mattie gun-shy when it came to relationships. Then Levi had plunked himself down on one of her bar stools, day after day, eating pie and drinking coffee and looking good enough to lick from head to toe.

He'd reminded her she was human with basic needs and desires.

Yeah, she wasn't a big fan of marriage, but she didn't have to abstain from *everything*.

Thus, a night of unrestrained sex with the gorgeous Delta Force soldier.

She couldn't regret it. But where did she go from there?

She stared at their entwined hands, unwilling to

untangle them, liking the way it felt to have a man hold her hand without trying to make her someone she wasn't.

"You should have woken me," he said softly, his tone warm and rich, spreading over her like melted butter.

"You were sleeping so soundly. I didn't have the heart to wake you."

He shook his head. "I don't think I've slept that well in years. But I would've liked to see you before you left." His fingers squeezed hers gently. "I hope you weren't running away."

She glanced away. "I might have been."

His brow dipped. "I'm sorry if I made you uncomfortable." He started to pull his hand away.

She didn't let go. "No. It's not like that." Her lips twisted into a wry grin. "I was a bit overwhelmed."

"We can take it slower next time."

She shook her head. "I was overwhelmed by how much I enjoyed our time together. Frankly, it scared me. Are we taking things too fast?"

"We can slow down," he said. "If you don't want to go out to dinner with me tonight, we can wait until you feel better."

"No," she said. "Really. I've been counting the minutes until I could see you again. I don't want to slow down. I just need to process what's happening."

"I get it. I didn't come to Colorado to start a relationship. It was possibly the last thing on my mind.

And it scares me, too, how quickly we came together. Maybe it would be smarter to slow things down." He stared at their joined hands. "But I don't want to."

She laughed, letting go of the breath she'd been holding. "Good. Whatever this is...we need to let it run its course."

He chuckled. "You make it sound like a case of the flu."

"Maybe it is," she said. "We both might get over it after the newness wears off." For her part, she doubted her burgeoning feelings for Levi would wear off anytime soon. She suspected they'd last indefinitely.

His lips quirking on the corners, Levi gave a subtle lift of his chin, aimed over Mattie's shoulder. "Don't look now, but the ladies at the bar are staring at us."

Mattie spun toward Joyce and Marcy, giving them a narrow-eyed glance.

Levi chuckled again. "I said, don't look, and what's the first thing you do?"

She laughed and faced him. "I looked."

"Do they always stare that hard?"

Mattie's lips twitched. "I'm sure we're giving them a show by holding hands in public. They will have it all over the county before the end of the day."

"Then maybe we should give them something more to talk about." A wicked gleam flashed in Levi's eyes.

Mattie's breath caught. "What did you have in mind?" Her voice came out breathy as if she was having a hard time breathing. Which was a fact. When she was around Levi, she found it difficult to breathe normally.

"A kiss," he whispered. "A full-on, no-holding-back kiss."

If she'd had trouble breathing before, she completely forgot how to suck air into her lungs after his words.

As Levi started to rise from his seat, Mattie's pulse raced. Her tongue darted out to moisten her suddenly dry lips.

The man was coming around the table. Still holding her hand, he brought her to her feet and tugged gently, drawing her closer.

Mattie barely registered the jingle of the bell over the diner entrance, announcing the entrance or exit of a customer. She was caught by an unrelenting force she couldn't break free of. Nor did she want to.

"Mattie McIntyre," a deep voice said behind her, jerking her out of the trance Levi's gaze had thrown her into.

Mattie looked over her shoulder at the older gentleman standing a few feet behind her. Her brow furrowed as she recognized him. "Chris?"

The attorney whose office had been on fire earlier glanced from her to Levi and back. The roadmap of wrinkles across his face seemed even more pronounced than usual. His face, smeared with soot, was no less professional. "We need to talk."

She pulled away from Levi's grasp, frowning. "Chris Malone, this is Levi Franks. Levi, Chris Malone, my attorney and friend."

Levi shook hands with Chris.

Mattie waited until he dropped Levi's hand before she said, "I heard your office caught fire. Is everybody okay?"

He nodded. "We made it out fine with minimal smoke inhalation. But my files..." he shook his head. "Every bit of paper stored in my office is burned."

She touched his arm. "I'm so sorry."

He drew in a deep breath and let it slowly out. "It's probably just as well. It's as good an excuse as any to retire, like I've been threatening for years. I'm seventy next month. I need to retire and enjoy my last few years."

"Oh, Chris, you're not old. You're going to be around a lot longer." She smiled. "But yes, you should enjoy your life. You've worked so hard for so long. You deserve a break."

He nodded. "And I will. But I didn't come to tell you I'm retiring. I have official business that concerns you." He looked past her to Levi. "I need you to come with me, or at least follow me. I have something I need to show you."

Curious, she tilted her head. "What?"

His lips pressed together as he glanced around the diner. "It's best if I show you...alone."

Deanna chose that moment to enter the diner. "Good morning, sunshine," she called out and stopped, her smile slipping. "What? Did I interrupt something?"

Mattie shook her head. "No. But I need you to cover for me for a little while."

"You've got it," Deanna said, her smile back. "Don't worry about us. We can hold down the fort as long as you like."

"Thank you." Mattie met Chris's gaze. "Are we walking or driving?"

"Driving," Chris said. "You can ride with me or take your own vehicle."

The intensity of Chris's words and demeanor had Mattie's gut tied in a knot. She trusted Chris with her life, but something about how he acted set her on edge. "Levi and I will follow you." She turned to face Levi. "If that's okay with you."

He nodded. "Absolutely."

The attorney frowned. "I'd prefer to meet with just you, Mattie."

She shook her head. "After what happened to Earl yesterday, I'd feel better having Levi with me. He saved my life yesterday. Whatever you have to say to me, you can say in front of him. I trust him."

Chris stared hard at Levi. "Okay." The older man

turned and left the diner, the bell over the door ringing loudly in the silence he left behind.

Levi cupped Mattie's arm. "We'd better get moving if we want to keep up with Mr. Malone."

The attorney climbed into a sleek white SUV and backed out of the parking space.

Levi opened the passenger door of his truck for Mattie.

She got in quickly, and he rounded the front of the cab and slipped behind the steering wheel.

The attorney had pulled out onto Main Street before Levi started the engine of his pickup.

"The man doesn't waste time, does he?"

Mattie's frown deepened. "He's never been this... intense before. His office caught fire earlier today. That has to weigh heavily on his mind."

Levi shot a glance her way. "Caught fire?" He pressed hard on the accelerator, quickly catching up to Chris.

Mattie explained about the smoke and the fire trucks.

They passed the burned-out remains of Chris Malone's attorney's office. Seeing the building blackened with soot made Mattie's stomach roil.

"I wonder what Chris is going to show me."

"Has he ever acted this way before?" Levi asked.

She shook her head. "No. He's usually very open and straightforward when he needs to communicate legal matters."

Chris led them out of town, turning off the main highway onto a smaller farm road and then onto a gravel road.

"Where the hell is he taking us?"

"I don't know." Levi's jaw hardened. "I have a pistol in the glove box. Could you take it out and lay it on the console within my reach?"

Mattie's eyes widened. "Chris is harmless."

"Maybe so, but we don't know where we're going or if Chris is the only person waiting at the destination. I'd rather be ready for anything."

Mattie opened the glove box, removed the pistol and laid it on the console beside Levi, her hand remaining on the weapon to keep it from sliding.

The gravel road turned into a rocky, rutted path barely wide enough for their vehicles to traverse.

When they emerged into a clearing, Chris had come to a stop and was getting out of his SUV.

Mattie looked past Chris to the arched opening into the base of the mountain behind him. "What the…"

Levi took the gun and got out of the truck.

Mattie slid from her seat, down to the ground, and closed the distance between her and her attorney. "What is this?" she asked, pointing to the mountain behind Chris. "Why did you bring me out here?"

Chris sighed. "I didn't want to say anything while we were within earshot of anyone in Fool's Gold."

Mattie's frown deepened. "What's wrong? You're scaring me, Chris."

He stepped aside and waved a hand toward the tunnel. "This is one of the entrances to the Fool's Folly Mine."

Mattie looked from Chris to the mine's entrance and back. "Okay. What does it have to do with me? Why all the secrecy?"

"Mattie, Earl came to me yesterday morning and asked me to write up his will. I told him it would take a couple of days. He insisted I do it while he waited. He insisted I make it simple and get it recorded immediately, even walking with me to the county courthouse to have it recorded."

Mattie jammed her hand into her pocket, her fingers closing around the golden nugget, her heart beating so fast, her vision blurred and her head spun. "I don't understand."

"Mattie," Chris met and held her gaze, "Earl left this to you. You're the new owner of the Fool's Folly Mine."

CHAPTER 8

L<small>EVI'S BLOOD</small> iced in his veins, and his hand tightened around the pistol.

Chris's eyes widened, and he raised his hands. "Look, I'm not the one who left the mine to her," he said. "I'm just the lucky guy who had to tell her." He turned to Mattie. "Trust me. I'm not any happier about it than you are."

Mattie's face had paled as she stared at the mine's entrance. "Why would he do that? I'm no relation to him."

Levi stepped beside Mattie and slipped his arm around her, steadying her.

She leaned into him, her body trembling.

"He said his niece hadn't been out to see him, check on him or spit on him since his brother brought her out to Fool's Gold when she was three years old. She's thirty-three now and never attempted to get to know her uncle, even though she's his only living relative."

"Never?" Mattie shook her head.

"He sent her birthday cards every year for the past thirty years. Each had a twenty-dollar bill inside. Some years, he went hungry to put that twenty in the card and mail it to her. She never called to thank him. He said you, Mattie, showed him more kindness and love every time he came to the diner than his niece ever had. For that reason, he said he left a gold nugget as a tip on your table in the diner."

Mattie brought her hand out of her pocket and opened it to show Chris the nugget Earl had left. "He left it for me." Tears slipped down her cheek.

"Earl said he was afraid the curse was catching up to him and that he had to get his affairs in order to make sure his niece didn't end up with the mine. He'd worked too hard for too long to leave the mine to someone who didn't give a rat's ass about him. He wanted you to have it," Chris said. "Now, I don't know whether that's a blessing or a curse. You'll have to make that decision. I've informed you of Earl's will. It was the last thing I could do for him. He appeared to be at peace once it had been signed and recorded."

"What happens next?" Mattie asked, her tone flat, her gaze on the dark tunnel entrance.

"The mine will go into probate for a few months.

Then it will be yours. We can go over all the legal stuff when you're ready."

"But your office..." Mattie's brow puckered. "If everything burned, wouldn't the will have burned as well?"

Chris's lips twisted. "I'm old and somewhat untrainable, but Linda keeps me straight. She scans every document that comes across my desk before it can be filed. Everything is backed up to an offsite database. I have copies of everything I've done over my lifetime as an attorney. And since it was recorded at the courthouse, a copy will be there as well." His brow dipped low. "Whether you believe in the curse is up to you. Earl didn't blow up his home. I didn't set fire to my office, and I'll bet those who owned the mine before Earl and died of so-called natural causes aren't dead because of some curse. I didn't want to do the will for Earl, but I knew if I didn't, he would find someone else to put it together. Please, Mattie, be careful. I'm worried you'll be next."

"I'll be careful," she said.

Chris nodded. "I'm heading back to town. You can follow me or stay. Either way, I'm glad you brought Mr. Franks and his gun for protection. As soon as word gets out that you inherited the mine, your life will no longer be safe."

The attorney left, his SUV kicking up a cloud of dust that lingered in the air like the pall hovering over Mattie as she digested the attorney's revelation.

Levi's arm tightened around Mattie's shoulders. "Are you all right?"

Mattie shook her head. "I'm not sure. I went from owning a diner to owning a diner and a gold mine. What the hell am I going to do with a gold mine?"

"I don't know," Levi said. "I wouldn't go inside until we have flashlights and let someone back at the lodge know where we're going. I don't relish falling down a shaft never to be found."

"Like Earl's Uncle Al?" Mattie shivered. "I bet he was pushed. And I might be the next victim to fall down a shaft or have my apartment destroyed with me in it." She turned into Levi and leaned her forehead against his chest.

He wrapped his arms around her, not wanting to hold her back but not letting go. "As long as the killer is still out there, I'll protect you."

"I've fought tooth and nail for my independence." Mattie tipped her head back to look up into his eyes. "Do you know how hard it is to rely on someone else?"

"I don't want to control you, Mattie. That's not what protection is about. My training in Delta Force taught me the value of teamwork. No man is an island. You have to be able to rely on your team to have your back." He tipped her chin up so that she looked into his eyes. "We're a team of two. You can't look over your shoulder all the time to see what's behind you. That's my job. I'll have your back."

"And as part of our little team, I'll have yours," she whispered.

He bent to brush his lips across her forehead. "I don't believe in curses, but I do believe there are bad people out there who could hurt you. Stay close to me at all times. Twenty-four-seven."

She nodded. "Maybe I should get a gun?"

"Do you know how to use one?" he asked.

Mattie shook her head. "No."

"I can take you to the firing range Jake and Gunny set up on the Lost Valley Ranch. Until you're familiar with a weapon, I don't recommend carrying one. You'd end up shooting yourself instead of the bad guys."

Her lips pressed into a thin line. "I'm a quick learner. I'd appreciate it if you didn't patronize me because I'm female."

"Whoa." Levi held up his hands. "I don't care if you're male, female, or a purple, polka-dotted alien. You're better off without a gun if you don't know how to use it. I had a guy on the range put his bullets into the magazine backward. Range control yanked his ass off the range so fast his head is probably still spinning four years later. And I had a new female recruit who was a natural and fired expert on her first trip to the range. However, when she cleared her weapon, she almost blew her foot off. Weapon familiarity comes with a lot of practice, not a fifteen-minute, this-is-a-gun briefing."

Mattie chuckled. "Okay, okay. I get your message loud and clear."

Levi drew in a deep breath and let it out slowly. "Sorry. I've seen some stupid shit happen with weapons."

"I can only imagine," she said. "Someday, I want to learn how to use one properly *and* take the time to practice." She raised her eyebrows. "Does that meet with your approval?"

He sighed. "You don't have to have my approval. You're a smart woman. I'm betting you'll learn quickly, like you said, and do it all right."

"In the meantime, what can I do to defend myself?" she asked.

"Are you trained in any kind of self-defense?" he asked.

She shook her head. "My ex-husband was emotionally and verbally abusive, not physically. I intended to take a course in self-defense, but I got busy building a business."

"And didn't take time out for self-care." Levi nodded. "And your business is thriving. You've done an amazing job."

"I always say the best revenge is success." She lifted her chin. "I never claimed to be perfect. Part of the reason I worked so hard and was willing to sacrifice so much was to be a success and show my ex-husband that I could do it. I could be more than arm candy. I have a brain, and I'm using it. I'm not stupid."

Levi frowned. "Did he tell you that you were stupid?"

Mattie nodded. "He did it so many times he almost had me convinced he was right."

"Bastard," Levi muttered. "You're the smartest, nicest and most compassionate person I know." He gripped her arms and stared down into her beautiful face. "He was an idiot. You deserve so much better."

"I know," she said. "As soon as I realized it, I left him, filed for divorce and haven't looked back except to compare where I was to where I am today." She pushed her shoulders back. "I'm making it on my own, damn it. I don't *need* a man to support me. I don't need a man at all."

His lips twisting, Levi raised his hands. "I guess that makes me obsolete. Does that mean our date is off?"

"No way. You can't back out on me. I have the perfect dress picked out." She touched his arm. "I said I don't *need* a man in my life. I'm perfectly capable of making my own way in the world. I don't have to be dependent on anyone."

When Levi opened his mouth to say something, she touched a finger to her lips. "I might not need a man, but if I allow a man into my life, it won't be because I need him or have no other choice. It'll be because I *want* him in my life."

Mattie cupped his cheek in her palm. "Right now,

I want you in my life. Not because I need you…" Her voice dropped to a whisper. "But because I *want* you."

"Please tell me you'll tolerate me long enough to let me take you out to dinner at least once. I promise to be on my best behavior." He winked.

"Now, I feel like a terrible person. I haven't dated since college, where I met my ex. I'm out of practice. I guess you've already gathered that I hold my independence close to my chest and don't ever want to lose it again."

"I have no plans to take it away. I feel honored that you want to be with me, even if it's only for dinner. And you should hang onto your independence. No woman should have to be in a miserable relationship because she feels like she has no other choice. I find strong woman…" his smile slipped across his face, "sexy."

Mattie blushed. "Good. Because I'm never going to be the mouse I was before."

Levi crossed his arms over his chest. "Now that we have the matter of your independence settled and understand the difference between want and need, we can go out on a date, fully aware of the boundaries."

Mattie laughed. "I promise I'm not always this difficult."

"You're not difficult. You know what you want, and you don't settle for less. I'm okay with that. More than okay. I think you should go for what you want.

I'm glad I'm on the side of your wants and not your needs."

He held out his hand. "We should shake on it."

Mattie looked at his hand. "A handshake?"

Levi slipped his hand behind her back and pulled her close until his hips touched hers. He lowered his lips to within a breath of hers. "Better?"

Mattie wrapped her hands around his neck and deepened the kiss.

Her mouth was warm, wet and wonderful.

Levi lost himself in her, claiming her mouth and tongue in a long, sensuous kiss. When he finally came up for air, he stared down into her eyes. "I don't think I can get enough of you."

Her eyes fluttering softly at half-mast, she sighed. "I *know* I can't get enough of you. It scares me more than the terror of my first kiss under the football bleachers."

"Scared? Of me?"

She shook her head. "No. I'm scared of how quickly I'm falling for you."

His heart warmed at her confession. "I'm having the same misgivings. I haven't been on a real date since before I got married. What if whatever we're feeling wears off within a few weeks? I don't want to hurt you when I leave."

Mattie's lips quirked upward on one side. "Or when I boot you out the door?"

He nodded. "Or when I boot *you* out the door."

"Can we agree not to boot anyone without first discussing it?" Mattie asked.

"Agreed. We don't want to get blindsided, fall apart and leave a messy emotional wake for everyone to navigate, right?" He dipped his head once. "Let's do this."

"Do what?" She rolled her eyes.

"Step inside and check it out."

Mattie glanced toward the mine. "Yeah, I feel like we should at least go inside. After all, I own it now. Not too far inside. We don't want to fall down a shaft because we can't see it. That would make us like the girl in the horror films who goes back into the mansion with the serial killer. We're not too stupid to live."

"Deal." Levi waited for her to make the first move. When she didn't move, he shook his head. "Are we going inside?"

With a shrug, Mattie answered. "I was waiting for you to make the first move."

Levi chuckled. "I was waiting for you."

"For Heaven's sake." Mattie took his hand and marched toward the entrance. "Let's get this over with so that we aren't so wishy-washy when we come back with flashlights."

She stepped into the tunnel entrance, careful not to trip over the steel railroad tracks leading into the mine.

Levi held tightly to her hand to keep her from

going past the limited light edging around the corners of the tunnel entrance.

Standing in the sunlight, looking into the dark, gave Levi a ripple of apprehension.

"Earl said he could hear whispers in the mine shafts." Mattie cocked her head to one side and closed her eyes. "I don't hear anything."

"Maybe you're not close enough," Levi offered.

Mattie snorted. "I'm as close as I want to be."

"You make me laugh with one foot in the mine and the other in the sunshine." Levi stared down at her light red hair. The sunshine turned it a burnished copper. It made him uneasy standing so close to the cursed mine. Not because of the curse but because someone was using the curse to get around without getting caught.

"Okay," Mattie said. "I've seen all I can see without a flashlight. We can head back to town and see how many people already know about my inheritance."

As they made their way back toward the tunnel entrance, the rumble of loose gravel sliding down a hill reached them where they stood. The sunshine at the entrance faded into a murky haze as dust, gravel and rocks slid across the tunnel's opening. Already, the pile of stone and gravel was knee-deep and getting deeper.

"It's a landslide," Levi shouted. "Run!" He grabbed her hand and ran for the opening as it quickly disappeared beneath the landslide of dirt and gravel falling from the mountainside above.

Using his body to shield Mattie, he tried to push through the pile of debris. When he made no headway, he half-threw Mattie over the top at the same time as he dove through the narrowing opening.

Rocks pummeled his back and glanced off his head, neck and back.

Mattie rolled to the bottom of the rockslide, came up on her feet and raced away from the mine.

Levi tucked and rolled until he reached hard ground. Gathering his feet beneath him, he pushed himself upright and ran to catch up with Mattie.

Not until they were well away from the tunnel entrance did they stop running and stand back to watch as the rocks kept coming. Had they not escaped when they had, they would have been trapped in the mine until someone had dug them out.

Levi turned to Mattie and pulled her into his arms. "Are you okay?"

She nodded and pushed her dusty hair out of her face. A trail of blood oozed down the side of her face from her temple to her jaw.

"Hey. You've been injured." Levi tucked a strand of dirty hair behind her ear and studied the wound. "You're going to have a bruise there. Maybe even a black eye."

"Beats being buried alive," she said. "Can I claim it as a battle scar?" She smiled up at him. Even with her skin and hair covered in thick dust, she was still amazing, funny and beautiful.

He bent to kiss her and came away, spitting out dirt.

Mattie giggled and then laughed. Finally, she doubled over, holding her sides.

Her laughter made Levi smile, then chuckle and, finally, laugh out loud. A full, belly laugh that made his sides hurt.

Tears of mirth created tracks down their faces.

When the laughter faded, Levi's brow furrowed. He studied the side of the mountain overhanging the now-buried tunnel entrance. "Why after all the years of the tunnel being open and operational, was there a landslide at the exact moment you and I stood inside the shaft?"

Mattie's smile faded as she, too, stared at the mountainside. "The curse?"

Levi met her gaze with a steady one of his own. "Let's get out of here. I don't trust that there won't be another strange *coincidence*. One that could prove more destructive than a random landslide that almost buried the new owner of Fool's Folly Mine."

He slipped his arm around her and hurried her to his truck, helping her up into the passenger seat. "Are you sure you're not hurt anywhere else?"

She shook her head. "Just bruises." Her brow knitted. "What about you? You took the brunt of most of the falling rocks."

"I'll be all right. We need to get back to town." He rounded the truck and slid into the driver's seat. Moments later, they were bumping along the old mining road leading to the farm road and, finally, the highway that ran through Main Street.

As they entered Fool's Gold, Mattie turned to Levi. "We should probably go by my apartment and rinse off the dust before we go to the diner. Do you have a change of clothes?"

Levi nodded. "I keep a gym bag with jeans, sweats and a couple of extra T-shirts behind the back seat."

"I know it's strange," Mattie stared out the front windshield, her brow dented, "but I don't want to give the killer the satisfaction of knowing he almost had us. He will have to work a lot harder than a landslide to take me down." Her eyes narrowed, and her jaw tightened. "I sure as hell am not going down without a fight."

"I'm going to make sure you don't go down at all. But if it's a fight he wants, it's a fight he'll get."

CHAPTER 9

LEVI CALLED Jake on the way into town to give him a brief update. He also insisted on stopping by the bank, as dirty as they were, and placing the gold nugget in a safety deposit box.

Finally, they made it to the apartment.

Mattie never realized just how small her apartment was until Levi walked in.

His broad shoulders filled the space and then some, making the one-bedroom apartment she'd been contentedly living in feel no bigger than a closet.

Everywhere she turned, he was there, stirring her blood and raising the temperature of the room as well as her body.

As much as she'd rather stay there and make love through the afternoon and into the evening, they needed to get cleaned up and back to the diner as soon as possible.

"Do you have the gut feeling our killer will show up at the diner today if he hasn't already been there day after day?" she asked.

Levi nodded. "Like an arsonist hanging around the fire he started?"

"Yes!" Mattie walked through the room, she peeled her dirty shirt over her head. A cloud of fine dust rose from the fabric.

Levi stood near the apartment door. "Is this an invite, or are you just teasing me? I wouldn't dare assume anything."

"Seriously?" she asked, one eyebrow hiked.

"Sweetheart, you'll have to spell it out for me."

She glanced over her naked shoulder, unclipped her bra and let it fall to the floor. "What do you think?"

He grinned. "I think I'd like clarification. In this *me too* world we live in, a guy can't take anything for granted."

Mattie's lips twisted into a wry grin. "So much for vamping. Yes. This is an invitation. Yes, I want you to join me in the shower. And yes, you're right to ask. Now, are you coming, or do I have to extend a written invitation?"

He gripped the hem of his T-shirt and dragged it over his head, tossing it on top of Mattie's. The combined cloud of dust rose to the ceiling. "Maybe we should deposit our clothes straight into the washer," he suggested.

"Agreed." Mattie led the way to the laundry closet, hidden behind bifold, louvered doors. She flung open the door, backed away and stepped out of her jeans. "I can't get over the amount of dust all over our clothes and skin." She shoved her shirt and jeans into the front loading washer. Then she shimmied out of her panties and bra and dropped them in as well. When she turned, her eyebrows descended. "You've got some catching up to do. I want to get to the diner as soon as possible. So, chop-chop!"

He laughed as he shucked his boots, socks and jeans. Then he scooped Mattie up in his arms, carried her into the adjoining bathroom and set her down on the tile floor.

"I don't think I've ever had a man carry me to the bathroom, or anywhere else for that matter." She stood before him. Naked. "I think I like it."

"Good, because I like carrying you." He winked and nodded toward the shower. "You get to set the temp."

She reached in, turned on the faucet, adjusted the temperature and stepped beneath the spray. With her face in the water, she couldn't see Levi, but she knew when he stepped in behind her. The heat from his body warmed her.

His hands came up around her, slick with soap bubbles that he rubbed all over her skin from the top of her head to the tips of her toes and some sexier places in between.

She turned to face him, lathered her hands full of suds and returned the favor, washing away the dirt and dust of the landslide from every inch of his sinewy body.

They'd been lucky to make it out of the mine before the entrance had been completely blocked. They were luckier still that the larger rocks and boulders had missed them. They could have been crushed or severally injured if just one of the massive boulders had slid free of the mountainside and landed on them.

Once their bodies were clean, Mattie couldn't resist tasting Levi's moist skin. She brushed her wet lips across his and traced a path from the corner of his mouth down his chin, neck and lower to the broad expanse of his chest. She paused at one of the small brown nipples, swirling her tongue around it before nipping it gently.

He smoothed his hand over her wet hair and down her naked back to her buttocks.

Then he cupped the backs of her thighs and lifted her, pressing her against the cool tile wall. "How soon do we need to be at the diner?"

"The sooner, the better," she said and pressed a kiss to the side of his neck. "Within reason," she added and nipped his earlobe.

Levi laughed and pressed her harder against the

wall, his fingers finding her clit and stroking her there until she cried out her release.

He liked how she responded to him, how her body came alive under his fingertips. The woman exhibited no inhibitions, her sexual prowess strong and virulent, making him want to make love to her there in the shower until the water turned cold and he could barely see straight.

Alas, they had a mission.

Find and neutralize the man responsible for the deaths of the previous mine owners and, potentially, theirs.

When Levi hesitated, Mattie sank onto the tip of his cock. "What's wrong?"

"Protection," Levi said. "I used what I had last night."

"And you didn't replenish today?" She shook her head. "Does that mean we're done here?"

"Traditionally, yes." Levi grinned. "We don't have to be traditional."

Her lips curled upward. "You're right. We don't have to follow tradition. We can forge our own paths. We just have to be smart and careful about it."

She lowered herself over him, letting his cock enter her.

"How is this protection?" he asked.

Mattie sighed. "It's not. And, sadly, we need to get going. But it feels so right."

He closed his eyes, his cock pulsing inside her.

She wanted to keep going, to let him have her unshielded, unprotected.

Mattie liked how it felt for him to be with her without any barriers between them.

But it was crazy to let her guard down that much. What if she got pregnant?

Her heart fluttered, and her gut tightened.

A baby.

An intense ache started in the pit of her belly and spread into her chest.

What would it feel like to carry a baby inside her? To have Levi's child growing in her womb?

Mattie froze. She hadn't gotten pregnant with her ex-husband.

He'd considered that fact her fault. She had to be the one who was infertile, unable to have children. A failure, yet again.

What if he'd been wrong, and he had been the one who was shooting blanks all along?

Mattie wanted children. She'd hoped by having a child with her ex, that he would come to love her, even with all her flaws.

When she hadn't conceived, he'd blamed her and berated her every chance he could get.

Mattie wanted a child. Hell, she wanted more than one. With her biological clock ticking, she doubted some strapping young sperm donor would offer up his services. And why would she go the route of having a sperm donor when this man stood in front of her in all his naked glory? She could have his baby.

The thought hit her square in the gut. How could she have thoughts of procreating with Levi when a killer was out there? And she was his new target.

"We don't have to do this now," Levi said.

Mattie sighed and leaned her cheek against his. "I want to," she said.

"But we need to get back to the diner," Levi finished. He lifted her off him and let her slide down his body until her feet touched the ground. "The killer might be right there, sitting in a booth, feeling pretty good about himself for causing that landslide. As much as I'd like to find some protection and make love to you, we need to locate the killer and take him down before he hurts anyone else."

Mattie slumped into him. "I know. It's hard to focus when you're being jerked back and forth. I don't want to hurt anyone, especially you."

"You're not going to hurt me. We'll muddle through this insane attraction we have for each other."

Mattie chuckled. "Insane about sums it up. I was perfectly happy being alone."

Levi smiled. "So was I."

"Until you." Mattie and Levi said at the same time.

Mattie met Levi's gaze and held it for a long moment, water streaming across their naked bodies. She leaned up on her toes and pressed a kiss to his lips. "You're right. We need to figure out who's behind the killings." She leaned back into the spray, rinsed once more then turned off the water.

They dried each other and dressed without talking.

Mattie's thoughts were on the diner and who might be there. She was eager to get there and see who would show up. After brushing the tangles from her hair, she slicked it back from her face and let it hang down her back in long damp strands. It would dry on its own. She didn't want to take the time to blow-dry and style.

When they were dressed and ready, they left her apartment, climbed into Levi's truck and drove the two blocks to the diner.

Mattie paused with her hand on the door handle, staring at the front of the diner. "Chris, you and I should be the only people who know I've inherited the Fool's Folly."

"Apparently, we aren't the only ones," Levi said.

"I see no reason to keep it a secret, especially after the landslide. Maybe we can lure the killer out by making him angry with me for flaunting my inheritance?" Mattie shrugged. "I mean, what else can we do?"

"I don't like that you're a target."

"Me either, but it is what it is. If I give him something to aim for, he might get sloppy and reveal himself."

Levi sat with his hands curled so tightly around the steering wheel that his knuckles turned white. "I only hope I'll be enough to protect you." He faced her. "You have to stay close to me at all times. I can't protect you if I'm not right there with you." He reached for her hand. "Promise me you'll stay close."

She nodded. "I will. Trust me. I don't want to face the killer alone." Mattie squared her shoulders. "In the meantime, I'll be watching everyone who walks through the diner's doors. The killer could be someone I see every day. It's frightening."

Levi squeezed her hand. "I've got your back."

She nodded. "Okay. I'm game."

Levi dropped down from the truck and rounded the front to open Mattie's door.

Usually, she would have gotten out without assistance. With an unidentified killer running loose, she wasn't excited about being around a lot of people.

"It feels weird," she murmured.

"What feels weird?" he asked as he closed the truck door.

"Going into the diner, knowing the killer could be walking among us. He could be a regular customer. I hate that I don't know who to trust anymore. This guy has been in Fool's Gold all this time, hiding in plain sight." A shiver rippled through her.

A van pulled into the parking space next to Levi's truck.

"Good afternoon, Miss Mattie," a cheerful voice

called out as Danny Fink got out of his service vehicle and crossed to join Mattie and Levi.

Mattie smiled at the friendly gas truck driver who serviced the area's propane tanks. "Hi, Danny. You're driving a van today?"

He nodded. "I drive the van when I'm on service calls to fix things. The truck when I'm refilling propane tanks."

A regular at the diner, he always had a smile and friendly words to say. The man was a solid representative of the company he worked for, polite and gregarious. He didn't know a stranger.

"I'm on break and thought I'd stop in for some coffee and a piece of your pecan pie." He held out his hand to Levi. "I don't believe we've met. I'm Danny Fink."

Levi gripped the man's hand. "Levi Franks. Nice to meet you."

Mattie stepped through the swinging door to the diner and held it for Danny. "Business a little slower in the summertime?"

Danny nodded. "A little. People still need fuel for their hot water heaters and gas stoves. I spend most of my days on the road between delivery stops." He shrugged. "Most people are nice to me, so I have no complaints. What about you?"

He walked with them across the diner's floor to the bar and took a seat. "I heard about what happened to Earl yesterday. I was sorry to hear he didn't make it."

Mattie stepped behind the counter, grabbed a mug and filled it with coffee. "Yeah, the fire chief suspects the gas line was tampered with, causing the explosion. You're in the gas business..." she tilted her head and studied the man, "how would one tamper with a gas line to the point it might explode?"

Danny shook his head. "They could do it any number of ways. I heard of a family injured in a horrific fire because their puppy chewed through the gas line." The gas man sighed. "Sadly, the puppy didn't make it."

"That is sad and scary." Mattie cut a piece of pecan pie, laid it on a plate and handed it to Danny. "I don't suppose you were anywhere near Earl's neighborhood before the explosion, were you?"

"Actually, I was filling Mrs. Rhodhe's tank a couple of blocks away when the explosion happened. The ground shook where I stood." He met Mattie's gaze. "I heard you were there when it went off."

Mattie nodded.

Danny pointed to the cut on Mattie's forehead. "Did you get that from the explosion?"

Mattie shook her head. "No, but I got other bruises. Can I get anything else for you?"

"No, thank you. This will hit the spot and hold me over until dinner."

"How are your dogs?" Mattie asked.

Danny grinned. "Spoiled, fat and happy. I built a fence around my backyard so they can run without being on a leash."

"I'm sure they love it." Mattie spied the city manager, Randal Whitley, her attorney, Chris, and the speculator who rented a desk in Whitley's office. "Please, excuse me." Mattie smiled at Danny, grabbed mugs and the coffee pot and hurried across to the three men who chose a booth in the far corner.

As she passed Levi, she cast him a quick glance, glad he was there. Knowing Levi had her back, she wasn't nearly as nervous about being in the same room with a serial killer.

She stopped at the booth where the three men sat. They leaned across the table, speaking quietly. When she approached, they all smiled as one and leaned back, their conversation on hold.

"Good afternoon, gentlemen," Mattie said. "What can I get for you?"

Whitley gave her his best campaign trail smile. "Just coffee for me."

"Water for me." Chris met her gaze and held it a moment longer than usual.

"Coffee." The speculator pushed to his feet and held out his hand. "We haven't been properly introduced. Name's Jeff Rankin. I'm a precious metals scout. I hear you're the new owner of the Fool's Folly Mine."

"So I'm told." Mattie's eyes narrowed as she shook

the man's hand. "Mattie McIntyre." Her gaze shifted to the attorney.

Chris raised his hands, palms up. "I didn't tell them. But you know how it is in small towns. Word travels fast."

Mattie's lips pressed together. "Yes, it does."

Jeff pulled a business card out of his breast pocket and handed it to her. "I know it's all new, and you need time to digest the fact you now own a mine, but when you have a minute, give me a call. I'd like to discuss your plans for the mine."

She glanced at the card, then tucked it into the back pocket of her jeans. "Thank you."

Randall leaned back in his chair. "Jeff knows his stuff. He helps broker deals between individuals and mining corporations. He's good at what he does."

"I'll keep it in mind." Mattie left and returned a few minutes later with their drinks.

As she turned to go back to the counter, the bell over the door jingled violently.

Mattie spun to see who had blown through the door so fast it nearly knocked her bell off.

A petite, bleached blonde stormed in, planted her fists on her hips and spoke loudly, "Mattie McIntyre?"

Mattie frowned. "I'm Mattie."

The woman marched across the floor, raised her hand and would have slapped Mattie but for Levi springing to action.

He caught the woman's wrist and held it suspended.

"Let go!" She tugged hard, trying to escape his hold. "Let go, or I'll scream."

"I'll release you when you promise not to hit my client," he said.

The woman glared at him and then at Mattie. "That conniving hussy stole my inheritance."

He stared down at her, still holding onto her wrist. "I don't care if she stole your car, your dog or your husband. I won't let you assault my client."

The blonde snorted. "She stole my mine. I should've inherited the Fool's Folly." She jabbed a finger at Mattie. "Not her. You have no right to the mine. You're not even related to Earl Farley."

Mattie shook her head. "I didn't ask for it."

"That's a lie!" The woman tugged again at her captured arm. "Fine!" she said. "I promise not to hit her."

Levi released her wrist but stayed close, his body between the woman and Mattie.

Mattie hid a grin. She could take the blonde, but it was fun to see Levi doing his protector thing.

The blonde sneered at Mattie. "My uncle wouldn't have left the mine to a stranger. What did you do, sleep with him?"

Mattie gasped. "Most certainly not."

"You must be Kathleen Smith, Earl Farley's niece." Chris had risen from his seat and stood behind the blonde. "Miss McIntyre wasn't a stranger to your late uncle. She has been nothing but kind and caring toward Earl. From what he told me, you haven't attempted to contact him in years, even though he attempted to stay in touch with you at least once a year."

Kathleen turned on Chris. "Who the hell are you to judge me?"

"I'm the attorney Mr. Farley came to when he wanted to draw up a will."

Kathleen poked a finger at Chris's chest. "Then I need to sue you for malpractice for mishandling this case. My uncle could've been suffering from dementia, and you didn't even question his judgment?" Kathleen looked from Chris to Mattie. "This isn't over. That mine belongs to me, not this whore who swindled it from my uncle. Is she cutting you in on whatever gold comes out of the Fool's Folly?" Kathleen shook her head. "Fine. I'll hire my own damned lawyer and sue you both. You cheated my uncle, and you cheated me out of what was rightfully mine. I'll have your license, and you'll be disbarred."

"You'll spend a lot of money and won't get anywhere," the attorney said. "Earl was in his right mind. The Fool's Folly Mine was his to leave with the person of his choice. I wrote up what he wanted and had it recorded. The will, as written, stands."

Kathleen crossed her arms over her chest. "We'll see." She faced Mattie. "You will never own the Fool's

Folly Mine. It belongs in my family. This isn't over." She flipped her long, bleached-blond hair over her shoulder and marched out of the diner.

"Wow." Deanna stepped up beside Mattie. "That woman has anger issues. Good thing Levi stepped in when he did, or you'd have one hell of a bruise on your face."

Mattie smiled at Levi. "Thank you."

He dipped his head in acknowledgment.

"I was just about to call the sheriff to come get the woman." Randall Whitley held up his cell phone with 911 visible on the screen.

Jeff Rankin stood beside Chris, his gaze following Kathleen out in the parking lot. "Does she have a chance at changing the terms of her uncle's will?"

Chris shook his head. "Slim to no chance, but she could tie up the mine in court for months or years."

"I didn't ask for the mine," Mattie repeated.

"No, you didn't," Chris said. "It was Earl's wish that you get it. Like it or not, you're the new owner of Fool's Folly Mine."

Mattie's lips twisted.

Great. She'd inherited a mine.

With the mine, she'd also inherited a killer.

Yay…

CHAPTER 10

LEVI HAD BEEN RAISED NEVER to raise a hand to a woman. The moment Kathleen had called Mattie a whore, he'd come close to knocking the bitch off Kathleen's face.

All the time the niece had spewed ugly words and threats at Mattie, the diner owner and now mine owner, had stood quietly, her face a mask.

Mattie's assistant chef touched her arm. "You know, I can handle the lunch and dinner crowd. Why don't you get out of here? As soon as the rest of Fool's Gold hears you're the new owner of the Fool's Folly Mine, people will come out of the woodwork to congratulate you or to tell you what you should do with it. Some will just come to stare at the woman who inherited a mine from someone who wasn't even a relative. You're going to get all kinds of grief. Give yourself a day off and process."

Mattie grimaced. "It all seems so crass and heartless to congratulate me for inheriting property. Someone had to die for that to happen—a nice man who only wanted to be treated kindly."

Deanna wrapped her arms around Mattie. "I'm sorry about your friend. Earl was always nice to the wait staff and me. It's hard to believe he's gone."

Mattie glanced around the diner. "I feel guilty leaving things to you and the others."

"Don't. You work so hard and take on more than any of us could hope to accomplish. Give yourself a much-needed break."

Mattie's gaze met Levi's. "Okay. If Kathleen Smith shows up again, call 911. Our customers don't need to listen to her being ugly to me or anyone else."

Deanna nodded. "I'll make sure that doesn't happen. So? Are you going?"

With a nod, Mattie said, "I'm going."

Deanna smiled. "And I'm going back to the kitchen before someone gets hangry."

Mattie closed the distance between herself and Levi. "Are you okay with getting out of here?" she whispered.

He nodded. "I'd like to stop by the sheriff's office and see if they've made any headway on their investigation."

"Good," Mattie said. "I need something to keep me moving. Sitting still is never a good option for me."

"Come on." Levi held out his hand.

Mattie placed her hand in his, loving that he liked holding hands. Even more...that he liked holding hands with her. She left the diner and all the people inside, not concerned about being watched or the object of the gossip that was sure to ensue.

She grinned as she imagined the tongue-wagging.

Mattie has a beau.

Did you see Mattie holding hands with that man from the security firm that operates out of the Lost Valley Ranch?

Mattie held onto his hand until she had to let go for him to get into the other side of the vehicle.

She felt as if they were playing hooky from her livelihood. Usually, it would have made her anxious. She'd worked so hard to build her business, she hated leaving it to others to run. No one kept it as clean as she did. And she'd gotten good about knowing how much food to prepare and when to get it started.

Deanna had come a long way as well. She'd worked with Mattie almost as long as Mattie had been the owner. She could handle anything Mattie could and then some.

Even though the sheriff's office was only a block and a half away, they drove and parked out front.

As they entered the building, Levi asked, "Is Rachel West on duty?"

The woman behind the desk grinned. "You're in luck. She's just coming off her shift if you can wait a few minutes."

Mattie nodded. "We can wait."

Five minutes later, Deputy Rachel West emerged from the back of the building. When she spied Mattie and Levi, her tired face perked up with a genuine smile. "Mattie, Levi... Griff said you might head this way for an update." Her smile faded. "I'm sorry to report that we don't have much. The sheriff and I canvassed Earl's neighborhood. Most people were either at work or were old with limited vision."

"Anyone see anything around Earl's house?" Mattie asked, knowing Rachel would have shared information if they'd had some. Still, she had to ask.

"Not much. Most of the stay-at-home moms and retired residents were too busy to glance out the window.

"I need to get one more woman's eyewitness account. She was on her way to a doctor's appointment when I went through the neighborhood earlier today. If you'd like, you can come with me now."

"But you're off duty," Mattie protested. "Wouldn't you put it off until tomorrow if we weren't here?"

The deputy shook her head. "I'd go with or without you. It won't take long."

"Then yes," Mattie said. "We'd love to hear what she has to say."

"You can follow me. That way I'll go home instead of coming back here."

"We'll be right behind you." Levi held the

passenger door open for Mattie and helped her up into his truck. "How are you holding up?"

Mattie gave him a crooked grin. "I'm fine. I'm just trying to take it all in."

He closed the door and got in on his side. "I'm sure your head is spinning with the inheritance news."

She nodded. "Why did he do it? I wasn't any nicer to him than any of my customers."

"You were probably nice to him when he needed it most. Unlike his own blood relative." Levi shook his head. "She was a piece of work."

Mattie snorted. "If she thinks I slept with Earl to get him to leave me his mine, what will other people think?"

Levi shot a glance her way. "Do you care?"

"Not really. As long as it doesn't impact my business, I don't give a rat's ass. I've worked too hard to build my business to lose customers because of someone spewing lies about me."

"I'm betting your customers will rally around you no matter what lies are told. You're good with them. I know." He grinned. "As one of your customers, I don't come in just for good food. I come in for the welcoming smile and the way you make me feel like I've come home."

She reached for his hand. "Thank you. I do love the people who come to the diner."

"It shows."

Levi pulled onto Main Street behind Deputy West and followed her through the streets to the one where they'd gone to talk to Earl.

Mattie's heart pinched hard in her chest when she saw the wreckage of Earl's home, flattened by the explosion. Her eyes stung with tears she refused to let fall. Tears accomplished nothing.

If she wanted to honor Earl, she could do so by helping discover who had killed him and the others before him.

Deputy West parked her SUV by the curb and got out. She waited for Levi and Mattie to join her before she walked up a narrow path to the front door of a white cottage with green shutters.

"Who is it?" a shaky voice called from the other side of the kelly-green door.

"It's me, Miss Ada, Deputy Rachel West. And I have a couple of my friends with me. Do you have time to answer some questions?"

"Yes, of course." The locks clicked as the woman disengaged them and swung open the door.

A white-haired woman who couldn't be much more than four-feet-ten inches tall stood in the doorway, her shoulders hunched, her hand resting on a cane. "Please, come in." She moved out of the doorway to allow them to enter.

Deputy West entered first.

"Miss Ada Brown, this is Mattie McIntyre and Levi Franks."

The woman smiled. "Oh, I know little Mattie McIntyre. I used to babysit her when she was still in diapers. Now, look at her..." She reached up and patted Mattie's cheek. "She makes better meatloaf than I ever did." Miss Ada turned to Levi. "Mattie, is this your man? He's a looker."

Mattie's cheeks heated. "No, ma'am. He's my...friend."

Miss Ada looked from Levi to Mattie and back to Levi. "If I was fifty years younger..." She shook her head. "Don't be shocked. I'm old. Not dead." She winked at Levi.

Miss Ada waved them into the living room.

Deputy West perched on a wing-back chair. Mattie waited for the older woman to sit on the couch before she sat beside her.

Levi settled on the other side of Mattie.

"Miss Ada..." Rachel pulled a pad and paper from her uniform pocket, "the night Earl Farley's home exploded, did you see anything unusual around his place or in the neighborhood?"

The old woman's brow wrinkled. "Unusual?"

"Maybe people moving about, a strange vehicle you didn't recognize."

"Well, now. I was in my bath when the explosion happened, so I didn't see anything."

Rachel smiled. "It could have been anytime during the day. Were you outside at all or looking through the window?"

Miss Ada tilted her head. "I was outside watering my plants on the porch. Then I sat in my rocking chair and had a cup of tea."

"That's good." Rachel nodded encouragingly. "Did you see any strangers on the street? A vehicle that you didn't recognize?"

The old woman touched a finger to her chin. "There was that yellow sports car that roars up and down the street every so often. I think Anita Donahue's grandson drives it. He usually races past, only, this time, he had to slow down when the propane delivery truck pulled out in front of him."

"Did you see any strangers walking around Earl's house?" Deputy West persisted.

Miss Ada shook her head. "Not that I could recall. There was a man jogging by in shorts and a T-shirt. I didn't recognize him. Oh, and a woman walking one of those designer dogs. A golden doodle or some such nonsense." She sighed. "I'm afraid I'm not much help."

"No, Miss Ada, you're helping a lot," Deputy West said. "Is that all you can recall?"

The old woman nodded. "I'm afraid so."

Rachel pulled a business card out of her pocket. "If you think of anything else, no matter how inconsequential it might seem, call me."

"I will. I'm so sorry about Mr. Farley. He wasn't home much, working on that mine of his, but he always waved when he passed my house. Sometimes,

I'd invite him in for a meal. The man looked like he could do with a good meal." She blinked up at Mattie and Levi. "You will stay for tea and cookies, won't you?"

Mattie touched the woman's frail hand. "I'd love to another time. Tonight, I have some things to take care of."

Miss Ada nodded. "I understand. We all have our busy lives. But if you ever feel like slowing down, stop in. I can always make a pot of tea and keep fresh cookies in my cookie jar."

Mattie squeezed the woman's hand gently. "That sounds lovely. I'll do it."

"You are the spitting image of your pretty mother." Miss Ada touched Mattie's hair. "She had the same fiery red hair and a smattering of freckles across her nose. I was so sorry to hear of their passing."

Mattie's chest tightened. "Thank you." She missed her parents. Especially when she faced particularly challenging situations like her divorce, and now, having inherited a cursed mine.

Deputy West stood. "Again, thank you for your time, Miss Ada."

Miss Ada struggled to stand.

Levi leaped to his feet, took her elbow and helped her up from the couch.

She met the deputy's gaze. "You'll let me know when you catch the man who killed Earl, won't you?"

"Yes, ma'am." Deputy West glanced around the older home. "Is there anything we can help you with before we leave?"

Miss Ada smiled. "No, thank you. I have everything I need where I can get to it. But thank you for asking."

Mattie hugged the little woman. "I'll be back for that tea and cookies."

The old woman patted Mattie's arm. "I'll understand if you don't make it. You're a very busy woman with a business to run."

"You know you're always welcome to come to the diner as well. I have meatloaf on the menu every day of the week."

"Thank you for the invitation. I don't drive anymore. If I want to go anywhere, I have to schedule a trip with my granddaughter or the old people's transport. Maybe my granddaughter could take me there sometime soon." She walked with them to the door, shuffling along with her hand on her cane. "Thanks for sitting with me. I don't get many visitors."

"Thank you for the information. We hope to catch this guy soon," Rachel said. "Goodbye, Miss Ada."

"I'll see you soon," Mattie said, making a mental note to schedule a visit on her calendar before she got caught up in everyday life. Miss Ada was a sweet woman who enjoyed company and probably didn't get many visitors.

Deputy West walked with Mattie to Levi's truck. "Are you going to be all right?"

Mattie shot a glance toward Levi. "Yes."

"I understand Levi's been assigned as your protector." The deputy dipped her head. "Only the best come to work for the Brotherhood Protectors. You're in good hands."

Mattie smiled. "I know."

Levi glanced toward the wreckage of Earl's house. "Have they conducted an investigation of the house?"

Rachel nodded. "It was a break in the gas line, just as the fire chief suspected."

"Is the area off limits?" Levi asked.

"I don't think so. It might not be safe to poke around. They did secure the gas lines, but the structure is compromised."

"I'd like to look around," Levi said.

"Let me touch base with the sheriff." Rachel stepped away, pulled out her cell phone and made a quick call. She was back a minute later. "He said you could poke all you want. They had to move rubble to get to Earl's body. They've scheduled a demolition crew to clean up the site next week."

"We won't stay long," Levi said. "Then we'll head out to Lost Valley Ranch."

"Griff and I might be out there later," Deputy West said. "I need a shower before I go anywhere."

After Rachel West left, Mattie walked while Levi

drove his truck and parked near what was left of Earl's place.

Mattie was hesitant to step into the house. Some of the walls were still standing. Most of the roof had collapsed. What was left of the ceiling appeared precarious at best.

Levi stepped through what had been the front door. The door itself had been blown off its hinges and lay on the lawn several yards from the house.

"This appears to have been the living room." He moved into one of the rooms with half a wall still standing. He bent and lifted boards and drywall to peer beneath.

Mattie noticed that the large section of drywall he held had a picture or map taped to it. "Hold up what you have in your right hand," she called out and moved as close as she could without stepping onto the house's foundation.

He lifted the patch of drywall and looked over the top to the side she was staring at. "What is it?"

Mattie studied the paper taped to the sheet of drywall with duct tape. "I'm not sure. I think it might be some kind of hand-drawn map."

Levi turned the piece around and brushed dust off the image. "I think you're right. It appears to be some kind of maze or..." he looked up, "a drawing of the tunnels inside an old mine."

"The Fool's Folly?"

"Would have to be." Levi carried the plaster sheet

to his truck, folded up the back seat and laid the map on the floor. He moved back to the house and dug through the rest of the debris in what might have been an office or small bedroom. After sifting through a few more rooms, Levi left the house and joined Mattie where she stood on the littered lawn. "Let's get to the Lost Valley Lodge. I want Jake to see that map. I'll also send a photo of it to Swede."

Mattie climbed into the passenger seat and buckled her belt. Levi slipped behind the steering wheel and drove away from Earl's neighborhood, heading out of Fool's Gold to the Lost Valley Ranch.

Mattie craned her neck to see the map on the back floorboard. "A map of the mine shafts would come in handy. It appears fairly intact. I wonder if it was the only one."

"I didn't see any others buried in the rubble," Levi said, "but that doesn't mean there weren't more."

"So, besides the potential mine map, what did we learn today to get closer to finding Earl's killer?" Mattie crossed her arms over her chest and stared through the windshield at the highway in front of them.

"For one, we learned that you are the new owner of Fool's Folly Mine. Which I'm not happy about."

"You and me both," she said. "Might as well paint a bright red target on my back."

"Right." He continued, "We learned that someone attempted to bury us alive at that tunnel entrance, leading me to believe he already knew you were the heir."

Mattie tapped her finger to her chin. "Or he's just trying to scare people away—and he did a pretty good job of it. At least with me."

"We also learned that Miss Ada changed your diapers." Levi grinned.

Mattie's face softened. "I *will* go visit her as soon as the danger has passed."

"We learned there was a yellow sports car that had to slow down to avoid a white gas truck, a man jogging and a woman walking a golden doodle," Levi said.

"And it was confirmed the explosion was due to a breach in the gas line entering the home." Mattie sighed. "It's a lot, but not enough. I'm not sure we're on the right track. Nothing seems to fit together."

Levi shook his head. "Hopefully, some of the others will see a pattern I'm just not seeing yet."

"Having the mine's map will help when we venture in," Mattie said. "I think we need to take guards to stand at the entrance to make sure no one tampers with the tunnel, the hillside or anything else that could get us trapped inside the mine."

"I don't like the idea of going into the mine. Even if we're fully equipped with lanterns, those tunnels were carved out over a century ago." Levi's brow furrowed. "We don't know the condition of the supports or even if they have supports in some of the tunnels."

"I have a feeling that the nugget Earl gave me has a lot to do with why someone is killing the owners. If we can find Earl's source of that nugget, we'll know for sure. I'm hoping the map will lead us there."

"And if we go on this hunt for Earl's gold vein, we could lure the killer out into the open."

"Finding Earl's pot of gold, or vein, in this case, might come at a cost," Levi warned. "Earl paid with his life. How much are you willing to pay?"

CHAPTER 11

LEVI DROVE BACK into Fool's Gold and then headed out the other end of town to Lost Valley Ranch.

The sun had dipped below the tops of the mountains, casting the terrain into the deep shadows of dusk, blending into the darkness of night before the stars blinked to life in the heavens.

Mattie's suggestion that they try to locate the source of Earl's gold nugget disturbed Levi.

Earl had spent over a year searching through the tunnels, sacrificing time he could have spent enjoying the sunshine, all in the pursuit of instant riches.

Levi snorted.

Instant riches. Ha!

How many hours had Earl spent beneath the surface? More than Levi wanted to.

He parked in front of the lodge and dropped down from the truck.

Mattie didn't wait for him to open her door. She met him at the front of the truck and slipped her hand in his. "If you don't want to explore the mine, we don't have to."

"I don't like the idea. Not at all." His hand tightened around hers. "I keep thinking of the owner who'd been pushed into a vertical shaft. I don't want that to happen to you." He lifted her hand to brush his lips across her knuckles. "I like you and want more time to get to know you." He could even be falling in love with her. The last woman he'd loved had died. Years passed before he could swim to the surface of his grief. If he let himself love Mattie, and she died because of some stupid curse...

Mattie brought his hand to her lips and pressed a kiss into his palm. "I'm not going anywhere without you. If you don't want to go into the mine, I understand. Especially after the landslide today. I don't relish being trapped in a tunnel for any length of time. I also don't plan on dying anytime soon. I have too many plans for the future. Plans I hope will include you."

Levi pulled her into his arms, crushed her mouth with his and drank her in like a man dying of thirst. The more he was with her, the more he wanted to be with her.

She was exactly what had been missing in his life, and he hadn't even known it.

When he came up for air, he leaned his forehead against hers. "You make me hungry."

She laughed. "I can cook something for you."

He shook his head. "Not that kind of hungry. The kind of hungry that fills the soul."

She smiled up at him. "Are you going all poetic on me?"

He grinned. "You bring it out in me."

She leaned up on her toes. "And you're not half bad."

He set her at arm's length. "Come on, let's show the team what we found and get their take."

Levi pulled the tunnel map affixed to the piece of drywall out of the back floorboard and carried it into the lodge.

"Just the people I wanted to talk to," Jake called out from the dining room. He carried a mug of coffee. "Some members of the team have gathered in the basement. We've been hearing crazy rumors coming out of Fool's Gold. We were hoping you could clarify." Jake frowned. "What have you got there?"

"Let's get to the basement first. Then we'll fill you in."

Jake led the way through the dining room, kitchen and then down the stairs to the basement.

Several men gathered around the large conference table. When Jake and Levi appeared, they turned as one.

Levi laid the map on the table.

"About time you showed up," John Griffin said. "I got some of the story from Rachel about your visit with Miss Ada."

"That's right," Tayo Perez chimed in. "Fill us in on what you've done so far."

Levi pulled Mattie forward.

"You've all met Mattie?" Jake glanced around the room.

"Damn right, we have," Cage Weaver said. "Best chicken fried steak in town."

"No. Best pot roast," Sawyer Johnson disagreed.

"You all have it wrong," Levi said. "Best coffee and apple pie."

The men all nodded.

"You've gone and done it," Enzo grumbled. "Now, I'm craving apple pie."

The other men laughed.

Levi gave a nod to Mattie. "Do you want to tell them, or do you want me to?"

"You can do the honors," Mattie said softly.

"Attorney Chris Malone had Mattie follow him to a location in the mountains where he informed her of Earl Farley's Last Will and Testament. He led us to the Fool's Folly Mine. Earl bequeathed the mine and everything he owned to Mattie McIntyre."

"Damn," Tayo swore. "They weren't even related, were they?"

Mattie shook her head. "Not at all."

"After Chris left us at the mine, Mattie and I ventured into a tunnel. Not far, but far enough. While we were just inside the entrance, a sudden landslide just happened to occur, sending gravel and rocks tumbling down over the tunnel's exterior opening. If we'd been any deeper in the mine, we wouldn't have gotten out in time."

Tayo made the sign of the cross over his chest. "It's the curse."

"Neither Mattie nor I believe there's a curse," Levi said. "A curse didn't sabotage the gas line going into Earl's house. A curse didn't cause the landslide that nearly trapped us inside the tunnel. A curse isn't going to target Mattie as the new owner of the mine."

Mattie lifted her chin. "A person, not a curse, is behind the previous owners' deaths. The man is a serial killer, and we're going to bring him to justice."

"How are we going to do that?" Jake asked.

Mattie grimaced. "We haven't gotten that far. The point is that this man cannot continue to kill. I plan on living a long, happy life. I refuse to let this man ruin my plans. I'm not done baking apple pies."

The men at the table cheered, "Here! Here!"

"Swede has been busy digging into the lives and relatives of the previous owners. Let's bring him up on the monitor."

Jake touched his fingers to a keyboard, and the monitor at the end of the conference table flickered on and Swede's face appeared.

"Good evening, gentlemen," he said. "We have quite a turnout for Levi's assignment, I see."

"We're all for one and one for..." Tayo shrugged. "You get the idea."

Swede chuckled. "I do. You must be Mattie McIntyre, the new owner of the Fool's Folly Mine. I'm Axel Svenson, aka Swede."

Mattie nodded. "Nice to meet you."

"What have you got, Swede?" Levi asked.

"I researched the lives and deaths of the previous owners of the Fool's Folly Mine back four years to when they started dying off at an alarming rate, starting with Andrew Brown, dead owner number one. One of two sons born to Martha Davis Brown and Robert Brown. Robert Brown owned the Fool's Folly Mine. The mine had pretty much played out in the early 1920s. Robert Brown wasn't that interested in mining. He found his calling as a science teacher. When he died from influenza, his oldest son, Andrew Brown, was twenty-nine years old. He'd been working as a janitor at a factory. When he inherited the mine, he quit his job and went to work searching for an untapped vein of gold.

"His mother married a man who, like Martha, had lost his spouse. He had a son he brought to the marriage. Andrew and his stepbrother worked the mine until Andrew's untimely death at the ripe old age of thirty-five.

"Enter dead owner number two. The mine

passed to the younger Brown son, who quit his job as a hotel concierge and went into the mine to find his fortune. Within a couple of months, he died, having lost control of his vehicle on a rainy mountain road.

"It was here where the Farleys entered the picture. Al Farley was Martha's older brother. Martha died of a stroke earlier that year. Since Martha's boys were both dead and her first husband had no siblings, her brother Al Farley inherited the mine. When Al fell to his death in one of the mine shafts, his nephew Earl got the Fool's Folly Mine."

"That's pretty much what we've heard," Levi confirmed. "So, is it true the only living relative that would have inherited the mine is Kathleen Smith?"

Swede nodded. "I did background checks on the relatives, and nothing came up for any of them except for Kathleen. She's in a bind, having overextended her credit cards. She's behind on her rent, car payment and now can't make her credit card payments. She's been turned over to a collection agency and really needs an influx of cash."

"No wonder she was so adamant about inheriting the mine," Mattie said.

"Did she even realize that in order to get gold out of it, you have to work it?" Tayo shook his head.

"So, we don't have much more to go on," Levi concluded. "Just one disgruntled niece."

"Did Earl owe anyone money?" Jake asked.

Swede shook his head. "Nothing showed up. The only relative in a financial bind is Kathleen."

"She might have been angry about not inheriting the mine, but I can't picture her as the serial killer," Mattie said.

"Who has the greatest motivation to kill the mine owners?" Levi asked. "Did you have a chance to look up the speculator, Jeff Rankin?"

Swede nodded. "I searched and didn't find any dirt on him."

Mattie sighed. "We're back to square one." She met Levi's gaze. "I don't know where to go from here. I can't put my life on hold for something that might or might not happen to me."

"No, but you can exercise caution."

"Then that's what I'll do."

Jake pointed to the table. "Do you want to talk about this hunk of dry wall you brought with you?"

Levi nodded, pulled out his cell phone and snapped a picture of it. "I found this in what was left of Earl's house. It appears to be a map of the mine tunnels. Swede, could you look into this. I don't know if it will help us with anything, but it could be useful when we explore the mine."

"I'll check it out," Swede said. "Send me that photo."

Levi forwarded the photo.

Mattie stood. "Gentlemen, thank you for your concern and time. I'd like to sleep in my own bed tonight since I have to rise at 4:30 in the morning to get things going in the diner."

"I'll keep digging," Swede promised.

"Thank you." Mattie's gaze met Levi's. "I'd like to go to my apartment and get some rest."

Levi nodded. "You can find me at Mattie's apartment until the killer is caught."

Jake touched Levi's arm. "We'll continue to monitor the situation and look for other connections. The best you can do for Mattie is stick to her like glue."

"I know. The problem is we don't have a single clue," Levi said. "The killer could be anyone." He sighed. "I'd better get going before Mattie gets too far ahead of me."

He followed Mattie out of the basement and out of the lodge.

She paced the length of the porch and back.

Levi stopped her by gripping her arms and staring down into her eyes. "Are you okay?"

She laughed. "Not really. I have a killer after me, and I have no idea who he is. Other than that, I'm fine. Just fine."

Levi chuckled. "Translated, that means you're not fine. Come on, let's take you home to your apartment so you can get some rest. You might feel better in the morning."

He cupped her elbow and led her off the deck and up into his truck.

They accomplished their drive back to Fool's Gold in silence.

When they reached Mattie's apartment complex, Levi checked their surroundings before he let her get down from the truck. No one jumped out of the bushes or from the other sides of vehicles. They made it to her apartment with no trouble.

"Are we being overly cautious?" Mattie asked as she dropped her purse on the counter and walked into the bedroom.

Levi followed. "No. If anything, we could be even more cautious. For now, get some rest. I'm here. I can sleep on the couch so as not to disturb you."

Mattie shook her head. "I'd rather you were right next to me. In my bed." She gave him a weak smile. "Not because I'm afraid, but because I'm selfish and know what I want. I want you."

Levi opened his arms and Mattie stepped into them. "I'm glad because that's what I want as well."

They undressed each other, not in a wild, sexy way but in a caring way that took into account the stress of the day.

They lay in her bed naked.

"Do you want to make love?" Mattie asked.

"More than you can imagine, but I think we both need sleep. We don't know what tomorrow will bring, and we need to be ready."

He pulled her into the curve of his arm and held her close until she finally drifted off.

She might not be in immediate danger, but she could be at any time.

Levi worried that he wouldn't be enough to protect her. The killer might wait long enough that they could become complacent, and then he'd make his move.

He'd have to be ready, on the lookout at all times. Levi smoothed a hand over Mattie's fiery red hair, loving the silky strands beneath his fingertips and the way her skin was so soft pressed against his. Yeah, he could get used to this. Hell, he wanted it. Could he risk losing his heart to her? She was a goddamn target. The risk was high and the threat real. She could die.

He couldn't handle it if she died.

His jaw hardened. Then he'd better, by God, not let that happen.

CHAPTER 12

MATTIE BARELY STIRRED the next morning, but Levi was already sitting up, reaching for the pistol he'd left lying on the nightstand.

"It's okay," Mattie said. "It's just time for me to get ready for work."

"Right," he said and laid the gun on the nightstand.

"You can sleep a few more minutes while I do my hair."

He scrubbed a hand over his face. "No, I'm awake." Levi laid back against the pillow.

Mattie smiled down at him. "Sure, you are." She kissed his cheek and would have rolled out of bed, but a muscled arm clamped around her, crushing her naked body against his.

His hard cock pressed into her belly.

She chuckled. "You *are* awake."

"Dreaming of you." He nuzzled her neck. "How soon do you have to be at work?"

"Mmm. I can spare a few minutes." Mattie ran her hand across his chest, sliding downward to take him in her grip.

His hips surged upward.

"Protection?"

"Next to the gun."

Mattie laughed and reached for the foil packet, her fingers brushing against his weapon's cool, hard steel. The matching hardness sent a ripple of fear and excitement through her body, setting her blood on fire.

Levi caught her hand in his. "Wait."

"But you're ready," she said.

"And you're not."

A second later, he had her flipped over onto her back. He began his campaign to conquer her senses by kissing and nibbling his way down her body, starting at the pulse wildly beating at the base of her throat. Quickly moving to her breast, he sucked the nipple into his mouth and pulled gently, flicking it with the tip of his tongue.

Heat swirled at Mattie's core, surging outward to the very tips of her fingers. Tension built, leading her to the peak until she launched into an orgasm so powerful it left her breathless.

How could one man find every erogenous zone

on her body, triggering a cataclysmic response that left her throbbing in its intensity?

She tugged on his arms, dragging him up her body until his lips captured hers in a kiss that penetrated her very soul. He'd touched her like nothing she'd ever experienced before.

Levi rose on his knees and rummaged in the sheets until he found the condom.

Mattie took the packet from him, tore it open and rolled the protection over his rock-hard erection. She paused long enough to fondle his balls. Then a need so strong washed over her.

She gripped his buttocks and guided him to her entrance.

Levi slid into her slick channel, slowly, excruciatingly careful, allowing her to adjust to his size and length. Once he was all the way in, he waited for a second, his breath arrested, his face tense.

Impatient for more, Mattie gripped his hips and moved him out and back in again, repeating the motion. With each stroke, she increased the speed.

Levi took over, setting the pace, pumping hard and fast in and out, the friction inside sending waves of heat washing over her body.

His breathing grew labored, and his face grew taut.

Mattie raised her knees, digging her heels into the mattress, her hips rising to meet his with every stroke.

Faster and harder, he powered into her, taking her to the edge and over it for the second time that morning.

Levi thrust hard and deep, his body clenching as he buried himself inside her and held steady, his release throbbing against her channel.

For a long moment, Mattie forgot to breathe, reveling in the incredible moment and intimacy she'd only ever experienced with this man.

As she drifted back to earth, she realized she'd done something she'd sworn she would never do again.

She'd fallen for a guy—so quickly and deeply there was no going back. After her first disastrous marriage, she hadn't wanted to commit to another man. She'd almost lost her identity with her husband. She'd been determined never to give up herself for another, ever again.

But with Levi, she didn't feel as if she was giving up a part of herself. With him, she felt as if she was adding to her identity, growing and becoming an even better version of the Mattie she could be.

Levi collapsed on top of her and rolled to the side, pulling free. "As much as I want to lie in bed with you all day, there are customers who would be highly disappointed if you didn't open your diner on time."

She sighed. "Don't get me wrong. I love my business and making people happy with the food I provide, but yeah. It would be nice to lie in bed all day just making love with you."

His lips quirked upward on the corners. "Tempted?"

"More than you know."

His lips twisted. "Yeah. You have a job, a business and customers with reasonable expectations." Levi smacked her thigh. "Get up. We'll shower and dress and get you to work. Mattie's diner will open on time despite our own late start."

As she dressed, Mattie's gaze wandered over to Levi. He had a beautiful body with several battle scars that only added to his appeal. She wanted to tell him she loved him, but she was afraid. What if he wasn't ready to hear it? What if he never wanted to commit to a relationship again? He'd lost his first true love. What if he couldn't love her as much as he'd loved his wife?

So many thoughts rushed through her head. She laughed when she realized none of them had to do with the more immediate danger of a serial killer who could be stalking her now that she was the owner of a certain cursed mine.

"What's so funny?" Levi asked.

Her cheeks heated. "Just random thoughts."

He pulled her into his arms and kissed her soundly. "I love that you laugh out loud for no apparent reason. I love that you smile at everyone who comes through your door. I smile just thinking about you."

She wrapped her arms around his waist and laid her cheek against his chest. "I love that you're like a rock firmly anchored in the ground...solid, unmovable and strong. You're not like a rock dangling over my head, at risk of falling at any moment and crushing the life out of me." She looked up at him and grimaced. "I really think you're better at waxing poetic than I can ever hope to be." She laughed. "What I mean is I like being with you. You make me feel safe, not smothered."

He kissed her again and nodded toward the door. "Ready?"

"I am. But if you keep kissing me, I'll be late."

He shook his head. "Can I help the fact you have very kissable lips?"

Mattie snorted. "Come on. I have to open the doors in less than thirty minutes."

Even though they were only a short walk away from the diner, Levi drove his truck and parked nearby.

Mattie unlocked the front door of the diner and stepped inside.

Levi followed her inside. "What can I do to help you get started?"

"You can pull the chairs off the tables and restock the napkin holders that need it. I'll be in the kitchen making biscuits."

He followed her into the kitchen, tested the lock on the back door and looked inside the supply closet.

Mattie's lips twisted. "No monsters in the closet?"

He shook his head. "Not this time. Don't open that outside door unless I'm with you."

Mattie frowned. "Do you think he'd come in here to attack me?"

"I think I don't want to take any chances or give him any opportunities." As he passed by her, he bent and brushed his lips across hers. "I'll be in the other room. You won't be in my line of vision. That scares me."

She smiled and held up a hand. "I promise not to open that door unless you're with me."

He left her in the kitchen and went to work setting the dining room chairs in order and filling napkin holders.

Mattie checked on him several times, needing to see him more than she needed to have him do another task.

By the time Levi was done setting up the dining room, Mattie had the first batch of biscuits in the oven. Their warm scent filled the air.

She took a moment to step out into the dining room.

Two men pushed through the front door, dressed in work overalls.

Her early shift waitress, Kylie, came in behind the men, a sheepish smile on her face. "Sorry, I'm late."

She hurried to shove her purse behind the counter and grab an order pad.

The diner filled quickly with the morning work crowd eager to eat and get to their jobs.

Mattie manned the kitchen, cooking order after order of oatmeal, French toast, eggs, pancakes, bacon and sausage.

Levi floated between the kitchen and dining room, helping where he could and getting out of the way when he couldn't.

Mattie's heart fluttered every time he entered her kitchen.

Well, he was a good-looking guy. The few times she peeked through the door, she noted the female customers vying for Levi's attention, blatantly flirting with him.

A stab of jealousy hit her square in the chest. What did she have to be jealous about? Levi had been with her the past two nights. If Mattie had her way, he'd be with her for many more.

Kylie came through the kitchen, lugging a big bag of trash.

"Why didn't you get Levi to help you with that?" Mattie asked.

"I hate to ask since he's not really an employee. Besides, it's my job." The pretty brunette lugged the bag to the rear door.

Mattie turned to rescue the eggs she'd been scrambling.

Moments later, Kylie came back through the rear door, grabbed an empty trash bag and went back out into the morning crowd.

The morning was particularly busy, stretching into the lunch rush.

Deanna arrived by ten-thirty, giving Mattie a moment to sit with Levi and eat a late breakfast.

"Is it always this busy?" Levi asked.

Mattie shook her head, staring around at the filled seats. "Not usually quite this busy."

Levi slathered jelly over the triangle of toast he held. "Do you think people are coming to see the woman who inherited Fool's Folly Mine?"

Mattie nodded. "I've had a few not-so-regular customers pop their heads through the kitchen door to congratulation me." She tilted her head to one side. "I don't know what to say. A man had to die for me to get the mine. 'Congratulations' doesn't seem to be the right sentiment."

"What time do you usually leave?" Levi asked.

"Depends on the workload. Some days I work all the way up to closing at 10:00 pm. Other times, Deanna manages the kitchen just fine without me."

Levi nodded. "We'll play it by ear."

"Have you heard anything from Swede or Jake?" Mattie asked.

"Nothing yet. I'll give them a call if they don't call me first."

Mattie's brows twisted. "Aren't you going to get bored hanging out here?"

"I might get out my computer and download the photo of the mine map."

"Good. I'd like to explore the mine further. It would be nice to understand the map before doing that." She glanced at her watch. "I'd better get back to work. It won't be long before the lunch crowd starts trickling in."

She re-entered the kitchen and got to work, making meatloaves, breading steaks and stirring ingredients into a stock pot to make her famous chicken gumbo.

Halfway through an incredibly busy lunch rush, Deanna cried out.

Mattie turned to find her assistant bleeding profusely from a gash in her hand. "Oh, sweetie, what happened?" She grabbed a clean dish towel and hurried over to Deanna.

"I got in a hurry and nearly sliced my thumb off."

"Let's rinse it first." Mattie led her to the sink, where employees washed their hands. She turned on the water and positioned Deanna's hand beneath a gentle stream. "That's a pretty deep cut. I think you'll need stitches."

Deanna shook her head. "I can't leave you here with this crowd."

"You can't work with that cut," Mattie reasoned. "In fact, you can't drive yourself to the clinic." Mattie wrapped the clean towel around the wound. "Keep pressure on it. I'll be right back."

She rinsed the blood off her hands and pushed through the swinging door into the dining room.

Levi sat at the counter with a laptop open in front of him. He glanced up as she came through the door.

All she had to do was wave once, and he was off his stool and standing in front of her a second later. "What's wrong?"

"Deanna cut her hand. She needs to be taken to the urgent care clinic for stitches. Could you do that? I can't leave now with a diner full of hungry customers."

Levi shook his head. "I can't leave you."

"I'll be fine. I'm not going anywhere, there are people all around me and no one would be stupid enough to make a play for me with a hundred witnesses around."

Levi frowned. "I don't like leaving you."

"The other option is for you to take over the kitchen cooking while I take Deanna to the clinic." Mattie cocked an eyebrow.

"Can't you call 911?"

"She's not having a heart attack." Mattie stared around at the full dining room. "I could have one of the waitresses take her, but then I'll be cooking and serving." She looked up at him. "I promise not to leave the building. I really will be fine."

Deanna came through the swinging kitchen door

and leaned close to Mattie to whisper, "The burgers need to be flipped, and the fries are done and need to come out of the grease. I tried, but I didn't want to bleed all over the food."

"I have to get back in the kitchen." She cast one more pleading look in Levi's direction.

"I'll take her," he said. He cupped the back of her neck and planted a kiss on her temple, taking the opportunity to whisper, "Stay inside, and don't trust anyone."

"I like it when you talk dirty to me," she said with a grin. "Too bad that wasn't talking dirty. Hurry back." She entered the kitchen in time to rescue the burgers, fries and a chicken fried steak.

Without Deanna to help, the work got hectic, and she fell behind by a few minutes. She knew the importance of getting orders out quickly for the lunch crowd that had to go back to work in a reasonable amount of time. All she could do was work harder, faster and more efficiently until the rush subsided.

Seven burgers, eight club sandwiches and three grilled cheese sandwiches, plus fifteen orders of French fries, six side salads and several bowls of gumbo later, the rush seemed to be never-ending.

The trash had piled up and was overflowing. She'd tied off two bags so far, and the third one needed to come out of the can before the contents spilled out yet again.

Mattie had hoped Levi would be back before she had to carry it out to the large bin behind the diner.

After she'd picked up garbage off the floor for the fifth time, she knew she had to do something.

It was at that moment the back door to the restaurant opened. Sunlight spilled through, silhouetting the man standing in the doorway.

"Oh, good. You're back. Could you take out the trash?" Mattie turned back to the grill to flip a grilled cheese sandwich before it burned.

"How did it go with Deanna's stitches?" she called over her shoulder.

When she didn't get an answer, she finished flipping the burgers and turned.

The man standing behind her wasn't Levi but Danny Fink, the gas man, and he was closer than Mattie anticipated.

"Oh! Danny." She pressed a hand to her chest and laughed. "I wasn't expecting you. What can I do to help you?"

"I was servicing the building next door and thought I'd stop in and say hello."

Mattie glanced over Danny's shoulder through the open door to the alley behind the diner. "How did you get in?"

"The door was unlocked."

"If you're hungry, you should go out into the dining room. A waitress will take your order."

"I'm not hungry," Danny said. "I wanted to talk to you."

Mattie moved burgers from the skillet to a warming tray. "What about?"

He gave her a tight smile. "I had a visit with Miss Ada this morning to light her pilot light on her water heater. She said you came by to see her yesterday."

"Yes, we did." Mattie pulled the basket of French fries out of the hot cooking oil and dumped them into a tray. She sprinkled salt over them. "How is she today?"

"Fine. She said you and that pretty deputy were asking about the explosion at Earl's place."

The hairs on the back of Mattie's neck rose to attention. "That's right." Her stomach clenched and her heart pounded. "Why are you here, Danny?" She started to turn to give Danny her full attention. Before she could, arms came around her, and a hand clamped over her mouth and nose. She was pulled back against Danny's chest.

"I need you to see something to understand."

Mattie struggled to free herself, but the man was much bigger than she was and twice as strong. His arms were like iron bands wrapped around both of hers, rendering them useless.

He lifted her off her feet and carried her toward the back door.

Mattie kicked and writhed to the best of her ability, but he held her too close. She couldn't touch the ground or get any traction to try and flip him over her back.

As she neared the door, she lifted her legs and planted them on either side, stopping Danny from moving forward.

He grunted, backed up and spun so that he walked out the door backward.

Once outside, he shoved her into the van parked at the back door with the gas company lettering on the door panels.

He got in with her and released one arm long enough to shove the sliding door shut behind him.

Mattie wiggled free of the arm holding her, ducked her head and plowed into Danny's gut. His big body stood between her and the door. She had to get past him to escape.

Danny grabbed for her arm and missed. He swung a meaty hand out and grabbed again, this time catching her hair. He yanked it hard, sending her flying into the side panel. Her head hit hard, stunning her long enough for Danny to flip her onto her belly and plant a knee in the small of her back.

She fought hard, screaming as loud as she could, but he outweighed her.

Danny pulled her arms up behind her and wrapped a zip-tie around her wrists, binding them together. He shoved a cloth in her mouth, then got up, moved to the driver's seat and drove away from the diner.

Mattie rolled onto her side, gagging on the filthy rag in her mouth. She tried to spit it out but couldn't manage to do that. With her wrists secured behind her back and the van weaving back and forth, she couldn't sit up.

She inched her way around the inside of the van, searching behind her for something rough to rub against to break the zip tie. All the while, her mind rolled over the fact it had been Danny Fink all along.

Hadn't Miss Ada said the yellow sports car had to slow down when a gas truck pulled onto the street?

Miss Ada.

Danny had been by to see Miss Ada. Dear Lord. Mattie prayed he hadn't hurt the old woman.

At first, Danny drove slowly, then increased his speed, probably as he cleared town and headed out on the highway. Soon, he slowed, turned and picked up speed again. Before long, he slowed again and turned off the highway onto a rutted, bumpy road.

Mattie bounced against the floor of the van until it came to a stop.

Danny got out, slid the door open and grabbed Mattie's feet. He dragged her to the edge of the van, stood her up, pulled the cloth from her mouth and spun her to look at the mountain in front of her. At its base was a boarded tunnel with a broken wooden sign hanging over the top. The words "Fool's Folly Mine" were engraved in bold black letters. It was a different entrance than the one Chris had shown her when he'd announced that she was the owner of the mine.

"We're here," Danny said, "where it all began."

Mattie's heart dropped to the pit of her belly. She'd known as soon as he'd grabbed her in the kitchen that it was him.

Danny Fink was the man who'd killed all the previous owners of the Fool's Folly Mine and was now working on eliminating her as well.

"Why?" Mattie demanded.

Danny snorted. "This mine should be mine."

"But you're not a member of the Farley bloodline."

"Neither are you, but Earl left it to you." His lip peeled back in an ugly sneer. "You've never put an ounce of effort into this mine. You don't deserve to own it."

"I didn't ask for it," Mattie said. "I don't want it."

"Maybe not, but I have to make sure you or anyone else don't get it and steal what's rightfully mine."

"Why do you think it's yours?" Mattie asked.

"I've worked it more than anyone in the Brown and Farley family. I worked harder than my step-brother Andrew. He never gave me half like always said he would. I worked hard and stashed away most of my findings in a stockpile of gold. I'll be damned if anyone else gets it."

"I don't want your gold. I don't even want this mine."

"As long as your name is on the deed, this property is yours." He pounded his fist into his palm. "Not mine."

"Fine. Let me sign it over to you."

"It's not that easy. I need a little more time to execute my plan."

"So, what are you going to do with me?"

His jaw firmed as he stared at the mine entrance. "What I did with the others. I eliminated them before they could take what belongs to me."

CHAPTER 13

LEVI DROVE Deanna to the clinic to drop her off with a promise to pick her up later. He waited long enough to make sure she'd be seen. A doctor came out, took one look at the cut and recommended that she go to the local Orthopedic surgeon to make sure she hadn't damaged anything beyond his ability to fix.

Levi glanced at the clock on his dash as he drove to the orthopedic surgeon's office and waited to make sure Deanna could be seen. He'd already been gone twenty minutes.

The unease in the back of his mind intensified with each passing minute.

Deanna finally told him, "Go. I'll find a way back to the diner or home. You need to be with Mattie."

"Are you sure?"

"If it's anything huge, they can call an ambulance

and transport me to the hospital." She shook her head. "I'm fine. Go."

Levi hurried out to the parking lot. When he turned his truck around to return to the diner, traffic on Main Street had come to a complete halt.

Sirens sounded in the distance, getting closer. A plume of smoke rose from somewhere ahead.

Levi couldn't even get out of the parking lot of the orthopedic clinic to circle around and take back roads to the diner.

While he waited, he called Mattie's personal cell phone. When she didn't answer, he wasn't too alarmed. He'd seen how hard she'd been working in the kitchen. She didn't have time to take a call. He just hoped she was okay and managing to get everything done she could with limited kitchen staff.

What bothered him most was that he didn't have his eyes on her. She wasn't even close enough he could get to her quickly on foot. What if the killer chose that moment to make his move?

Levi snorted. If he did make his move at that moment, hopefully, he would be just as stuck in traffic as Levi.

His cell phone vibrated in the cup holder. Levi picked it up, hoping it was Mattie returning his call. Instead, the display screen showed Jake Cogburn.

"Yes, sir," Levi answered.

"Got a call from our favorite deputy just now. She went over her interview with the old woman on Earl

Farley's street and fixed on one thing the woman told her that might be a lead."

"And that is?"

"She said something about a yellow sports car having to slow down when the white gas van pulled out in front of him."

Levi's pulse kicked up. "And?"

"Rachel did some calling around to the dispatcher at the gas company to ask if any service calls were scheduled in that area on that day."

Levi held his breath.

"There weren't any on that street or any of the adjacent streets."

"So, what was a gas van doing in Earl's neighborhood the day his own gas line was tampered with? Did the dispatcher know who was driving the van?"

"Fortunately, the company has GPS tracking devices that record everything about their vans, including where they go, how fast they travel and how long they stay at certain locations."

"Who was driving the van?" Levi repeated.

"Danny Fink," Jake said. "And Levi, there's something else."

Levi was already looking for a way to go cross-country to get out of the damned parking lot. "What else?"

"I was on a video call with Swede when Rachel's call came through. Swede picked up on the name

Danny Fink. Martha Davis Brown married Roland Fink whose son is—"

"Danny Fink."

"He was the stepbrother who worked the Fool's Folly Mine with Andrew Brown. Apparently, they had a falling out, and Andrew refused to let Danny back inside the mine."

"Let me guess," Levi said. "Andrew died shortly after the incident."

"Deemed an accident, Andrew fell and hit his head on one of the rails. Since he was working alone, no one found him until the next day. Investigators didn't find any signs of a struggle. They did question his former partner, Danny Fink. He was working that day at his new job."

"With the gas company," Levi concluded.

"Deputy West has an APB out for Fink and his work van. How is Mattie holding up?"

Levi's teeth ground together. "I don't know."

"What do you mean?"

Levi explained about Deanna's injury, the lunch rush, and now, the traffic backed up a mile away from the diner. "I'm about to go off-road and find another way around."

"Do it. With Danny Fink running loose and getting sloppier about how he does his victims in, there's no telling what he's capable of."

"That's what I'm afraid of." Levi put his truck into four-wheel drive, drove over the curb, down into a ravine and up the other side onto the road behind the clinic. Then he put the pedal to the metal and raced in the direction of the diner, praying his gut was wrong for once. Right then, his instincts were screaming that Mattie was in trouble.

As he pulled up to the rear of the diner, smoke billowed out of the back door. By the time Levi slammed his truck into park and leaped to the ground, the smoke was already dissipating.

He ran into the diner kitchen through the back entrance with his T-shirt pulled up over his nose.

Inside, one of the waitresses held a fire extinguisher aimed at the grill where charred burgers lay in little black circles.

"Where's Mattie?" he demanded.

The waitress shrugged. "That's what we'd like to know. One minute we're filling orders, and the next, the kitchen is empty, food is burning on the grill and our boss is missing." She crossed her arms over her chest. "Now you know everything we know. I thought she'd be with you. You two seem joined at the hip lately."

Levi pulled out his cell phone and dialed Jake. "Mattie's gone. Did you say the gas vans have trackers on them? Can you get the location of the van Danny Fink is driving today?"

"On it. I'll get back to you ASAP." Jake ended the call.

In the meantime, Levi had to cool his heels. There was no telling where Danny would take Mattie.

Levi's gut urged him to go to the Fool's Folly Mine. Danny seemed to be fixated on the mine and anyone who dared to own it.

He couldn't wait for confirmation. The sooner he got moving, the better chance of rescuing Mattie from the clutches of the serial killer.

Driving the back streets of Fool's Gold, Levi avoided the traffic-jammed Main Street and was well on his way out of town when Jake called back.

"He's at the Fool's Folly Mine. I sent you the pin of his location."

"He has to have Mattie. Why else would he be out at the mine."

"He's going to kill her," Jake surmised.

"Not if I can help it."

"I'm sending backup and equipment," Jake promised.

Levi ended the call, his heart pounding inside his chest so hard he could barely breathe.

He didn't want to think it but couldn't help himself. It was happening all over again. The woman he loved could die in the next few minutes, and he wasn't there to keep it from happening.

This was the reason he'd chosen to stay single. He couldn't take the crushing grief that had nearly crippled him when he'd lost his wife.

He couldn't do it again. Which meant Mattie couldn't die.

With his foot smashed to the floorboard, Levi raced toward the mine, praying he'd get there in time to save Mattie.

DANNY FINK SHOVED Mattie toward the boarded-up mine entrance.

She dragged her feet. Why make it easy for Danny? He wasn't going to show her any mercy.

When they were within a couple of feet of the boards nailed together across the tunnel, Mattie could see that they were nailed in such a way that the boards formed a kind of door.

Danny stepped forward and gripped the boards. As he shoved the door to the side, Mattie turned and ran in the opposite direction.

She stumbled over the rough terrain. Without her arms to balance, she tripped and fell, hitting her shoulder on the hard ground. Pushing past the pain, she rolled to her side, sat up, bunched her legs beneath her then stood.

She wasn't fast enough. Danny was on her before she ran two steps. He grabbed her arm and turned back toward the mine. "You're not going to get away," he said. "There's no escaping the Fool's Folly. Once it has you in its grip, it doesn't let go."

Mattie had to get away. The man was out of his

mind. "You know they're going to figure out you were the one to sabotage Earl's gas line. They probably already know and are looking for you now."

"All the more reason for us to descend into the mine. It's a maze very few can master."

"You can't hide in the mine forever," Mattie said.

"There is where you're wrong. Not only have I stockpiled gold, but I've also been collecting nonperishable goods, enough to last years. I have a source of water in the mine and enough kerosene for light to last however long I need to stay under."

His lips twisted. "The only thing missing was a woman to keep me company."

Alive in a maze of tunnels was better than dead at the bottom of a shaft. "So, are you going to let me live as long as I stay with you in the mine?"

Danny's eyes narrowed. "As much as I want the company, I'm not sure you're worth the risk. How do I know you won't kill me in my sleep?"

"Why would I do that when you're the only one who knows how to navigate the tunnels?"

Danny shot a glance her way, studying her as if looking for the truth in her words. "No, you'll run away and die."

"So, what's it going to hurt to keep me around for a while?" She had to stall him until she could find a way to escape or until Levi and his team could find her and take out this crazy man. Mattie wasn't ready to die. Not when she was falling in love with a man worth living for.

Yes, she was falling for Levi. He was everything her ex-husband wasn't. She wanted more time with the former Delta Force soldier.

A lifetime.

And babies.

She could picture Levi as the father of her children and the grandfather of their grandchildren.

Mattie had always wanted the kind of family she'd grown up in. Her parents had been loving and fun. The only thing that could have made her childhood better would have been brothers and sisters. She'd dreamed of having a family of her own someday with no less than four kids, a husband who would get down on the floor to play with them and who loved her enough to let her be the person she was meant to be.

Levi was all that and more.

Mattie would be damned if Danny Fink took that away from her. She wouldn't let him. There had to be a way to escape.

As Danny shoved her toward the mine, Mattie wiggled her wrists, twisting and turning them, hoping to break the zip tie. Nothing worked, and they were getting dangerously close to the mine's entrance.

Mattie pretended to stumble and dropped to her

knees. "Ow. I've turned my ankle. It hurts too much for me to walk."

"You're stalling." Danny grabbed her beneath one arm and attempted to haul her to her feet.

Mattie cried out and sank back to the ground. "I can't. It must be broken."

"Stupid woman," he ground out. Then he bent low, scooped her up and flung her over his shoulder.

Mattie kicked and twisted until Danny stumbled and finally let her fall to the ground.

"Enough," he yelled and backhanded her so hard she fell backward and hit her head against the hard ground. Her vision swirled and faded to black.

When Mattie came to, once again, she was slung over Danny's shoulder. The darkness surrounding them was only broken by the headlamp strapped to her captor's head.

They were in the mine.

Mattie had been unconscious long enough she had no idea where they were inside the mine. Danny could have taken any number of turns in the numerous passages crisscrossing the inside of the mountain.

He trudged through the tunnel, breathing heavily, straining under her weight.

When he finally came to a halt, he dumped her on

the ground and stood hunched over with his hands on his knees, sucking in air.

Mattie lay still, hoping he'd think she was still knocked out and praying she'd find something to cut through the plastic zip tie.

DANNY STRAIGHTENED and moved away from her. A moment later, a battery-powered lantern lit the room carved out of the mountain's interior.

Shiny veins reflected the lantern's light. In one corner was what appeared to be a wooden crate with a hasp and lock on it.

Danny fished in his pocket and pulled out a set of keys. He unlocked the box and threw the lid open.

From her position lying on the ground, Mattie couldn't see what was in the box.

Danny reached in and pulled out a rock about the size of a golf ball. Light glinted off its surface, just like the nugget of gold Earl had left for her.

He held it in front of her. "I know you're awake."

She opened her eyes fully. "Is that gold?"

He nodded. "And it's mine. I found it. I dug it out of the inside of this mountain. No one else knew where to dig. It was all me."

Behind her back, Mattie had located the sharp edge of a rock jutting out of the side of the cave wall. She rubbed the zip tie against the edge, pressing hard into it. "Where did Earl get the nugget he gave me?"

Danny's lip curled into a snarl. "He stole it from my stash. That's why he had to die." He stared at the shiny object and then placed it back in the crate.

All the while, Mattie sawed at the zip tie, pulling hard at the same time. It had to break. When it did, she'd find a way out of the mine and back to the surface.

"Once Earl found my box of gold, he stopped digging for himself. He stole that nugget from me and would've taken more if he could've carried it out in his pockets."

"Why did you let him live longer than the others?" Mattie asked.

"At first, he was searching for gold, digging into potential veins. If he'd found one, I could've tapped into it as well. Once he discovered my stash..." Danny shook his head.

"Why are you showing it to me?"

"You're not a threat. Not anymore. After today, there will be one less owner of the Fool's Folly. The curse will have taken yet another fool to her grave."

Mattie sawed harder. She was not going to be one more fool.

The zip tie snapped behind her, and her wrist broke free. She lay as she had been, waiting for Danny to turn back to his box of gold so she could make her move.

"The question now is where and how to dispose of your body." Danny turned away to place his gold back in the crate. As he pulled the lid over the box, Mattie rolled to her feet, shoved him hard toward the box and smashed the lid down on his head.

Danny slumped forward and didn't move.

Not willing to check for a pulse, Mattie grabbed the battery-powered lantern and ran away from the room and down one of the myriad tunnels, slowing when she couldn't see the ground in front of her, afraid of stepping into a vertical shaft.

Her best bet was to get far enough away from Danny then hunker down with the light off and pray he didn't find her. When he gave up, she'd work her way to the mine entrance and get herself out. Or wait until Levi and his team sent a search party into the mine to find her.

Though both options seemed almost impossible, she refused to give up. She had too much to live for.

Soon, she slowed and found a shorter tunnel that ended in a turn. She moved to the very back, ducked around a tight corner and extinguished the light.

Her breath caught in her throat at the utter darkness. No matter how her eyes tried to adjust, there was no light for them to adjust to.

She strained to hear sounds. The echo of footsteps sounded in the distance, along with a muttered curse.

Mattie remained silent, refusing to give away her position.

A hint of light flared at the corner of the passage.

Mattie shrank against the wall and held her breath until that light disappeared and the footsteps accompanying it faded.

She had no idea how long to wait until she attempted to find her way out. She only knew she couldn't let Danny find her first. He wouldn't be stupid enough to let her escape again.

CHAPTER 14

LEVI ARRIVED at the GPS pin location, where he found Danny Fink's gas company van. This was a different entrance to the mine than the one the attorney had brought them to.

He jumped out of the truck and then reached in to retrieve a flashlight and his gun.

The entrance appeared to be boarded shut. Upon closer scrutiny, Levi could see that the boards made a door that had been pushed to the side enough to allow entry.

Levi turned on his flashlight and entered the mine. He moved as quickly and silently as he could. Every so often, he stopped and listened. After several turns, he stopped and listened again. This time, he could hear the faint tapping of footsteps against the solid stone floor of the tunnel.

He turned toward the sound, hoping it was an echo bouncing off a wall in the opposite direction.

As the sound grew louder, Levi leveled his gun in front of him. He stopped and waited for the owner of the footsteps to come to him.

Five seconds later, a figure appeared in the tunnel, wearing a headlamp. "You shouldn't have done that," a man's voice said. "This time, I'm not messing around."

Levi held the flashlight to the side, away from his body. If the man was armed, he'd likely aim for the light.

"It's over, Danny," Levi said.

The man with the headlamp stood still for a long moment before he said, "I don't know what you're talking about."

"Yes, you do. The sheriff is on his way. We know you were the one who tampered with the gas line at Earl's house. You were the one who killed Andrew and Ross Brown, as well as Al and Earl Farley. Don't make it even worse by hurting Mattie."

Danny snorted. "If I did all that, how could killing Mattie make it worse? And where's your backup? I don't think anyone is coming. It's just you and me. Here. Now. I could hide your body just as easily as I've hidden Mattie's. No one will ever find either one of you."

Levi's chest tightened. Danny was lying. The man

had been looking for Mattie when he stumbled across Levi. She'd managed to escape him.

Hope surged. Good for Mattie. All Levi had to do was eliminate the threat that was Danny, find Mattie and get her the hell out of the mine.

"Do you know what happens when you fire a gun in a mine?" Danny asked. The bullet ricochets for several minutes until it loses its momentum or until it embeds itself in something that absorbs the blast. Something like flesh. "So go ahead. Fire away."

Levi hesitated. What if Mattie was nearby? The ricocheting bullet could hit her.

"Better yet, let me start the fireworks," Danny said. A shot exploded, the sound so loud as it echoed off the solid walls.

Levi dropped to the floor and covered his head as the bullet pinged off the walls, like a ball in a pinball machine.

It took a while, but the bullet eventually stopped.

"It's almost like Russian roulette. Let's do it again."

Levi inched closer to the man.

The second shot echoed loudly against the walls. The bullet hit the stone near Levi's head and bounced across to hit the other side of the tunnel before finally coming to a halt.

"They say three's a charm," Danny said.

"Yes, it is." Levi, tired of Danny's game, aimed for the light on Danny's head and pulled the trigger. The sound echoed off the walls, but the bullet never left the target.

Danny dropped to his knees then fell forward and lay still.

Levi rose to his feet. "Mattie?" He called out. "Mattie, can you hear me? It's Levi. You can come out."

He stopped calling out and listened. When he didn't hear anything, his gut clenched. Had Danny really disposed of her body?"

"Mattie!" Levi called out.

"I'm here," a faint voice responded. "Keep talking so I can find you."

"Be careful, darling. We've come this far; I can't have you falling into a vertical shaft. What would I tell our grandchildren? Your grandmother walks funny because she broke both legs in a gold mine?"

A chuckle sounded closer.

"Hey," he said. "What about your promise not to leave the diner while I was gone with Deanna? Do I have to worry about your ability to keep your promises?"

"I didn't leave by choice," she responded. A light appeared in the tunnel.

Levi's heart skipped several beats and then thundered against his chest. "Hey, babe."

"Where's Danny?" she asked, still moving forward. "He's here."

"Dead?" she asked, her voice not much more than

a whisper.

"Yes."

As she neared, she stepped over Danny's body and then flung herself into his arms. "I never doubted you'd find me."

"I wasn't going to give up. When you find something or someone good, you hold onto it with every fiber of your being." He tightened his arms around her. "I'm holding on."

She wrapped her arms around his waist and squeezed hard, still holding onto the lantern. "I'm going to put this out there. You don't have to say anything. You don't have to reciprocate, but I have to get it off my chest."

He laughed. "Go ahead."

"I love you, Levi Franks. I know it's crazy, and we haven't known each other long, but damn it. I love you." She hugged him tighter, dropping the lantern to the floor.

Levi's chest was so tight he could barely breathe, and his eyes stung. "Oh, baby."

"Please, if you don't feel the same, don't say anything yet. I'm determined to make you love me, one way or another. If I have to bake an apple pie every day for the rest of my life, I will. Just don't say you don't love me." She pressed her cheek against his chest.

"Sweetheart." He tipped her chin up until she looked into his face in the light from the lantern lying sideways on the floor. "I never wanted to love someone again. Losing the one you love is too hard. But you made me realize it's worth the risk to have the happiness and joy of loving someone, even if it's for a short time." He kissed her forehead and brushed his lips across hers. "I love you, Mattie. From the first bite of apple pie and your first welcoming smile, I knew I was home."

"Thank God," she whispered. "Speaking of home...how do we get out of here? I would love to go home and make love with you."

"I memorized the turns I made coming in. Come on. Let's get out of here."

His heart light, Levi led Mattie out of the Fool's Folly Mine, where they were met by members of his Brotherhood Protectors team and the county sheriff's department.

After answering a lot of questions and leading the sheriff to Danny's body and the crate filled with gold, they were finally allowed to leave.

They stopped by the diner to close and lock up, and then they went to Mattie's apartment, where they showered, ate a bite and fell into bed to make mad, passionate love.

Life was good, and Levi was glad Mattie was a part of his.

"I love you, Mattie."

"It's a good thing," she whispered, "because I love you, too."

EPILOGUE

Two weeks later...

"What are you going to do with all that gold they recovered from the mine?" Jake asked Mattie.

They sat around a large table in Gunny's Waterin' Hole. Half of Levi's team had gathered to celebrate solving the curse of the Fool's Folly Mine.

Mattie glanced at Levi. "I'm going to make some repairs to the diner, buy a house and donate the rest to a children's hospital."

"It was a good thing you two found that map. It made it easier to find Danny's crate of gold and the vein he'd been working," Gunny said. "Have you considered working the mine?"

Mattie shrugged. "I'm still thinking about it. I'm

just glad we were able to find Earl's killer and keep him from killing again."

Levi lifted her hand and kissed the backs of her knuckles. "I'm glad you weren't hurt in the process."

"So, does that make you two a thing?" RJ asked.

Mattie laughed and looked at the love of her life. "Does it?"

Levi nodded. "Absolutely. What do you say to getting married next weekend?"

Mattie blinked. "Is that a proposal?"

"No. Not quite." He dug in his pocket and extracted a box. Then he got down on one knee and opened the box. "Mattie, I love you with all my heart and want to spend the rest of my life with you. Will you marry me?" He smiled. "Now, that's a proposal. What do you say?"

Her heart bursting with happiness, Mattie flung herself into his arms. "Yes!"

The men and women around the table cheered and ordered another round.

"Not for us," Mattie said. "We're having tea and cookies in town with Miss Ada."

"We'd better go then," Levi said. "We don't want to be late."

He slipped his arm around her and led her out of the bar and into his life.

Mattie couldn't have been happier. Well, maybe a baby would add to their happiness, but that would come with time. She was sure of it.

DRAKE

IRON HORSE LEGACY BOOK #6

New York Times & *USA Today*
Bestselling Author

ELLE JAMES

DRAKE

IRON HORSE LEGACY

New York Times & USA Today Bestselling Author

ELLE JAMES

CHAPTER 1

"Damn," Drake Morgan muttered, checked his speedometer and repeated the expletive.

He hadn't realized he'd been going over the sixty-miles-an-hour speed limit until blue lights flashed in his rearview mirror. Lifting his foot off the accelerator, he slowed and eased to the side of the road, just a few miles from his destination.

A county sheriff's SUV pulled to a stop behind him, and a deputy dropped down from the driver's seat.

The tan, short-sleeved uniform shirt stretched taut over full breasts, the shirt-tails tucked into the waistband of dark brown trousers, cinched around a narrow waist with a thick black belt.

Definitely female. Too petite and pretty to be out patrolling the wild roads of rural Montana.

He lowered the window of his Ford F250 pickup,

reached into his glove box for the vehicle registration and insurance information she'd surely request and straightened.

"Sir, place your hands on the window frame," she said.

He raised his hands, one of which held the documents. The other he carefully placed on the window frame of his door, staring out the open window into the barrel of a pistol. He raised his gaze to the deputy's and cocked an eyebrow. "I have a concealed carry license," he warned. "My weapon is in the glove compartment. I'm unarmed at this moment."

"Just keep your hands where I can see them," she said, her tone curt, her eyes narrowed as she held the pistol pointed at his head.

"Can I ask why I was pulled over?" he asked in a calm, even tone, knowing the answer.

"You were exceeding the speed limit," she said. "If that's your title and registration, I'll take those. But no funny business."

"Trust me," he said with a crooked smile. "I've never been accused of being funny."

Her eyebrows pulled together to form a V over her nose as she took the papers he held out for her.

She studied the documents then glanced up. "You're not from around here," she said.

"No, I'm not," he said.

"Do you know how fast you were going?" she asked, all business, no smile.

Drake almost grinned at the seriousness of the young woman's expression and the way she stiffly held herself. "Over the speed limit?"

She snorted. "By at least fifteen miles an hour. In a hurry to get somewhere?"

"I was."

She shook her head, a hint of a smile tugging at the corners of her mouth. "And how's that working out for you?"

"You tell me," he quipped.

She was pretty in a girl-next-door kind of way with light brown hair pulled back in an efficient ponytail.

Drake stared up into her eyes, trying to decide if they were brown, gold or green, finally settling on hazel. To cap it all, she sported a dusting of freckles on her bare face. "You have my information, but let me introduce myself." He stuck out his hand. "Drake Morgan."

Her brow furrowed as she contemplated his extended hand. "I'm Deputy Douglas." She gave a brief nod, ignored his hand and stared past him into the vehicle. "Since you have a gun in the vehicle with you, you'll need to step out of the truck while I run your data."

Already late for the meeting with his team, their new boss, and this his first day on the job, he sighed, pushed open the door and stepped out with his hands held high.

"Turn around, place your hands on the hood of your vehicle and spread your legs," she said in a tone that brooked no argument.

He cocked an eyebrow. "I'm not a convicted felon. I owned up to the gun in my glove box. I'm unarmed and at your mercy."

Having stated her demand once, she held the gun pointed at his chest, unbending, waiting for him to follow through.

Rather than give her a reason to pull the trigger, he turned and complied with her command.

The shuffle of gravel indicated she'd moved closer. A small, capable hand skimmed over his shoulders, down his sides, around to his abs and lower. Bypassing his private parts, her hand traveled the length of his legs, patting both all the way to his ankles.

Out of the corner of his eye, he watched as she balanced her service weapon with her right hand as she frisked him with her left.

Finally, she straightened and stepped back. "Please stand at the rear of your vehicle while I run your plates and license."

He turned and gave her a twisted grin. "Told you I was unarmed."

She backed toward her vehicle then slipped into the driver's seat. Her fingers danced across a computer keyboard as she entered his license and registration data and waited.

Moments later, she got out of her work vehicle, weapon back in the holster on her belt, and strode toward him while writing on an official-looking pad. When she reached him, she ripped off the top sheet and handed it to him. "I'm only giving you a warning this time. Next time, I'll cite you. Slow it down out there. The life you endanger might not be your own."

With that parting comment, she spun on her booted heels and marched back to her vehicle.

"Deputy Douglas," he called out.

As she opened her SUV, she turned to face him, "Yes, Mr. Morgan?"

"You're the first person I've met here. Nice to meet you." He waved the warning ticket. "And thank you."

Her brow furrowed, and she shook her head as she climbed into the vehicle. Moments later, she passed his truck and continued toward the little town of Eagle Rock ahead of him.

Drake slipped into the driver's seat and followed at a more sedate pace. Hell, he was already late. What were a few more minutes? And it wasn't worth getting a full-fledged ticket. He was lucky she'd only issued a warning. She could've hit him hard with a speeding ticket, with the lasting effect of jacking up his insurance rates.

He owed her a coffee or a beer. Since she was the only person from Eagle Rock he knew besides Hank Patterson, he'd kind of like to get to know her better.

It paid to have the law on your side in these back-water towns.

Following the GPS map on his dash, he drove through town and out the other end, turning on the road leading to his destination.

Soon, he saw her, perched on the side of a mountain, her broad porches intact, her late eighteen-hundred charm shining through, despite the need for a good paint job and dry-rot repair.

The Lucky Lady Lodge clung to the side of the mountain, welcoming travelers in search of a quiet getaway in the Crazy Mountains of Montana.

From what Hank had told him, this lodge had been a place for the gold rush miners of the late eighteen hundreds to spend their hard-earned gold on booze and women.

After the gold had dried up, the Lucky Lady had become a speakeasy during the prohibition, with secret passages into the old mine where they'd made moonshine and stored the contraband in the mountain.

Drake had done some research on the old lodge. He'd found stories telling of days when mafia king-pins had come to conduct business while hunting in the hills or fishing in the mountain streams.

Fires had consumed hundreds of acres surrounding the lodge, missing it on more than one occasion by less than a mile. Throughout the years, the lodge stood as she had from the beginning, a little worn around the edges. Recently, she'd been damaged by an explosion in the mine. That's where Drake and his team would come in.

He looked forward to rolling up his sleeves and putting his carpentry skills to work restoring the old girl. He hoped that, like riding a bike, it would all come back to him despite the sixteen years it had been since he'd last lifted a hammer to build or repair anything more than a deck on the house of a friend. The summers he'd spent working on new home construction while in high school gave him skills he wouldn't have known otherwise and the confidence to try new things he'd never done.

Having joined the Navy straight out of high school, he hadn't had much need for carpentry skills. He'd focused all his attention on being the best military guy he could be. That had meant working his ass off and applying for the elite Navy SEALs training.

BUD/S had been the most difficult training he'd ever survived. Once he'd made it through, he'd been deployed on a regular basis to all corners of the world, fighting wars he thought were to help people who couldn't help themselves or protect his own country from the tyranny of others.

Drake snorted. He'd learned all too soon that war wasn't always for just causes. When he'd tired of putting his life on the line for the benefit of big business, he'd said goodbye to what had been the only career he'd ever wanted.

From there, he'd worked with Stone Jacobs as a mercenary in Afghanistan, leaving just in time before the US pulled out and left Stone and the last five members of his team stranded.

Rumor had it that former SEAL, Hank Patterson, had sent a rescue team to get Jacobs and his people out.

Since Afghanistan, Drake had refused to be another hired mercenary. He'd been drifting from one low-paying job to another. Nothing seemed to fit.

When Hank Patterson had called him out of the blue, he'd been working at a small diner in the backwoods of East Texas, dissatisfied with life, unable to fit into the civilian world and ready for any change that would take him away from the diner, the small-minded residents of the town and the meddling mamas bent on matching their single daughters to the only bachelor in town with all of his original teeth.

No, thank you.

Drake had been ready to leave East Texas.

When Hank's call had come, he'd been willing to listen and even come to Montana for a one-on-one chat with his old friend and brother-in-arms.

Hank had offered Drake a job as a Brotherhood Protector, a kind of security firm providing protection, extraction and whatever else was warranted for people who needed the expertise of someone skilled in special operations.

"I'm not interested in mercenary work," Drake had said. "Been there...done that."

"It's not mercenary work," Hank had said. "It's bodyguard, rescue and protective services for real people who need specialized help. We aren't working for big corporations."

Drake had been insistent. "Not interested. Got anything else?"

Hank chuckled. "As a matter of fact, I know someone who needs carpenters for a lodge restoration project. It's good physical work, and the lodge is worth restoring."

"Sounds more my speed," Drake said.

"Come out to Montana. See what we have here and make your decision," Hank had urged.

Drake had remained firm. "I'm not going to change my mind."

"Okay. I get it. But I want you to meet the guys who work with me and get their take on what we do."

"Fair enough," Drake said. "I'd still rather pound nails. It beats slinging bullets."

"I'll put you in touch with Molly McKinnon and Parker Bailey. They are leading the effort to restore the lodge. I've sent several spec ops guys their way already. You probably know some of them or know of them."

"I'm down for some renovation work with a team

full of former spec ops guys, as long as they aren't going to try to talk me into working for your Brotherhood Protectors." He thought he might have insulted Hank. "No offense."

Hank laughed. "None taken. Whichever way you lean in the job front, you'll love Montana and the little town of Eagle Rock."

Anything would be better than the close-minded, stone-faced inhabitants of the small East Texas town he'd worked in for the past six months.

"How soon can you get here?" Hank asked. "The other four SEALs are due to start on Monday morning."

"I'll be there," Drake had assured him.

"Great. See you then," Hank ended the call.

Drake had immediately given the diner his resignation, packed up his few personal items in his furnished apartment and left Texas. He'd driven for two days, stopping only long enough to catch a couple of hours of sleep at a rest area along the way.

When he rolled to a stop in the parking lot in front of the Lucky Lady Lodge, with the Crazy Mountains as a backdrop to the old building, he already felt more at home than he had anywhere else. Maybe it was because he was tired. More likely, he felt that way because he didn't want to move again.

As he stepped down from his pickup, he shrugged off his exhaustion. He could sink his teeth into this project. It beat cleaning years of grease off the diner's floor back in Texas.

With a new sense of purpose, he passed the large roll-on-roll-off trash bin, already half-full of broken boards, crumbled sheets of drywall panels, ruined carpet and damaged furniture. He climbed the steps to the wide veranda and entered through the stately double doors of the lodge.

Six men and a woman stood in the lobby, wearing jeans and T-shirts. They had gathered around a drafting table, all looking down at what appeared to be blueprints.

The woman glanced up. "Oh, good. Drake's here."

The others straightened and turned toward Drake.

As he studied the faces, his heart filled with joy.

He knew Hank from way back at the beginning of his career as a Navy SEAL. Hank had been the experienced SEAL who'd taken him under his wing and shown him the ropes of what it was like beyond BUD/S. Clean-shaven, he had a short haircut, unlike the shaggy look he'd acquired on active duty. The man had a few more wrinkles around his green eyes, but he was the same man who'd been his mentor so many years ago.

Hank stepped forward, holding out his hand. "Morgan, I'm glad you made it. You must've driven all night to get here."

Drake took the man's hand and was pulled into a

bone-crunching hug.

"Good to see you," Hank said.

"Same," Drake said. "It's been a few years."

Hank stepped back. "I believe you know everyone here."

Drake nodded, his lips spreading into a grin.

A man with dark blond hair, blue eyes and a naturally somber expression stepped past Hank and pulled Drake into another powerful hug. "Dude, it's been too long."

"Grimm," Drake clapped his hand on the man's back. "I thought you were still on active duty."

Mike Reaper, or Grimm as he'd been aptly nicknamed, patted his leg. "Took shrapnel to my left leg. It bought me early retirement."

Drake shook his head. "Sorry to hear that."

"I'm not. I was getting too old to play with the young kids. It was time for me to move on." He nodded. "I'm looking forward to getting my hands dirty with something besides gun cleaning oil."

"Move over, Grimm. My turn." A man shoved Grimm to the side. "Bring it in, Morgan."

A black-haired man with shocking blue eyes grabbed Drake by the shoulders and crushed him in a hug. "'Bout time we worked together again," he said. "When did we last?"

"Afghanistan," Drake said when he could breathe again. He grinned at his old teammate from his last tour of duty before leaving the Navy. "We took out

224

that Taliban terrorist who was cutting off heads for fun. How're you doing, Murdock?"

Sean Murdock stood back, smiling. "Better, now that you're here. Thought we were going to be Army puke heavy. We needed some bone frogs to level the playing field." He turned and dragged another man forward. "Remember this guy?"

Drake's brow furrowed. "Utah?"

The handsome man with the auburn hair and blue eyes smirked. "I prefer to go by Pierce. I like to think I've outgrown the Utah moniker."

Murdock laughed and pounded Utah on the back. "You'll never live down Utah. Once an uptight asshole, always an uptight asshole."

Pierce "Utah" Turner's lips pressed together. "Thanks." He held out his hand to Drake. "Good to see you under better circumstances than the last time we worked together."

Drake gripped the man's hand, truly glad to see him. "Taking mortar fire while trying to extract that Marine platoon was not one of our cleanest joint operations. You saved my life that day."

"And you returned the favor five minutes later," Utah said. "I'd call it even."

Drake glanced toward the last man he knew in the group and smiled. "Hey, Judge. You're a sight for sore eyes."

"Didn't think you'd remember me, it's been so long." Joe "Judge" Smith, former Delta Force Operative, was the old man of the group of men Drake would work with at the lodge. Like Hank, he'd influenced Drake when he was a young Navy SEAL fresh out of training. He'd been an integral part of the first joint operation of which Drake had been a part.

He'd hung back to provide cover fire for the team as they'd exited a hot zone. Judge had taken a bullet to his right forearm and had to use his left arm and hand to fire his rifle. The man hadn't missed a beat. He'd held on long enough for the entire team to reach the Black Hawk helicopters waiting at the extraction point.

When Judge hadn't been right behind them loading the aircraft, Drake had jumped out, determined to go back. He'd gone less than twenty yards when Judge had come running, dozens of Taliban soldiers on his heels.

Drake and the rest of his team had provided him cover until he'd dove aboard the helicopter. They'd lifted off under heavy fire and made it back to the Forward Operating Base without losing a single man. He'd made an impression on Drake he would never forget.

"What brings you to Montana?" Drake asked.

"Got tired of wiping the noses of baby Deltas," Judge said. "When I reached my twenty, I figured it was time to leave."

"I always wondered why they called you Judge," Drake admitted.

Judge shrugged.

Grimm laughed. "It came out of a barroom fight. Patterson didn't like the way a man was treating one of the ladies. When he told him to back off, the man asked him what he was going to do if he didn't." Grimm's lips curled. "He became the Judge, jury and executioner."

"You killed the guy?" the woman at the drafting table asked.

Judge shook his head. "No."

"He made him wish he was dead," Grimm said. "He almost got kicked out of Delta Force. If the woman he'd defended hadn't come forward to tell her side of the story, his career would've been over."

Drake glanced around at the men he'd fought with and shook his head. "Had I known we were having a reunion, I would've come sooner."

"I want each of you to know I would hire you in a heartbeat for my organization, Brotherhood Protectors, but you all have expressed your desire to fire nail guns, not Glocks. I haven't given up hope that you'll change your mind, but I respect that you want to try something different. And with that, I'll hand you over to your new bosses. Molly McKinnon and her fiancé, Parker Bailey, are from the Iron Horse Ranch." Hank waved a hand toward the man and the woman who'd remained at the drafting table. "They're the new owners of the Lucky Lady Lodge."

"For better or worse." The man took Drake's

hand. "Welcome aboard. I'm here to do the grunt work, just like you guys." He turned to the woman. "Molly is the brains behind the project."

Molly shook Drake's hand. "Glad to meet you. Now, if we could get started…"

He smiled. "Yes, ma'am."

She turned to the drawings. "We're in the demolition phase of this project. We have to clean up what was damaged in the mine explosion before we can assess structural damage," Molly said.

Parker added. "Each man has been assigned different areas to work, not too far from each other in case you run into trouble."

Molly pointed to the blueprint. "Drake, you'll take the butler's pantry and coat closet on the far side of the main dining room. The walls are cracked and crumbling. We need to get behind the drywall to see if the support beams have been compromised. Your goal today is to clear the walls on the mountainside of the rooms and any other walls showing significant damage."

Parker raised a hand. "I'll take Drake and Grimm to their locations."

Molly glanced toward the other three men. "The rest are with me. You'll find sledgehammers, battery-powered reciprocating saws, gloves and wheelbarrows staged in each of your areas. The power is off, so you'll have to use the headlamps on your safety helmets. The rooms against the mountain don't get much natural light." She handed Drake a helmet with a headlamp. "Thank you all for answering Hank's call. We needed as many hands as we could get for this project, and sometimes, people are hard to come by in small towns."

Anxious to get to work, Drake plunked his helmet on his head and followed Parker through the maze of hallways to the back of the lodge. They hadn't gone far before they had to stop and turn on their headlamps.

Parker continued, explaining what each room was as they passed doorways. He eventually came to a stop in front of a wooden door. "Grimm, this is your assigned area. Judge, yours is the next room. I'll be two doors down. If something doesn't feel right, get the hell out. We don't know exactly how much damage the explosion caused. I'd rather we err on the side of caution. The sooner we see inside the walls, the sooner we can get to work rebuilding."

"Got it." Grimm pulled on a pair of gloves, wrapped his hands around the handle of a sledgehammer and nodded. "Nothing like a little demolition to work out all your frustrations. Let's do this."

Judge entered the next room and found what he needed to get started. Parker moved on.

Gloves on, Drake grabbed the sledgehammer and went to work knocking big holes in the plaster on the back wall. Piece by piece, he pulled away the plaster and the narrow wooden slats behind it, exposing a couple of feet of the interior beams at a time.

Plaster dust filled the air, making it more and more difficult to see. Judge found face masks in the stack of supplies and pulled one on over his mouth and nose. He'd made it through half the back wall in less than an hour. If he kept up the pace, he'd have that wall done in the next hour. The other walls in the room had only hairline fractures in the plaster. Hopefully, that was a good sign that they hadn't been damaged to the point they needed to be torn down as well.

One thing was certain; they'd have to wait until the dust settled before they could assess the status of the support beams.

The banging on the wall in the next rooms stopped for a moment.

"Can you see anything?" Grimm called out.

"Not much," Drake responded. "My headlamp is reflecting off all the dust particles."

"Same," Grimm came to stand in the doorway, wearing a mask over his mouth and nose.

"Let the dust settle for a few minutes," Parker called out.

"Have you had a chance to find a place to live?" Grimm asked.

Drake shook his head, his light swinging right then left, bouncing off the dust in the air. "I just got to town and came straight here."

"I think there's room at Mrs. Dottie Kinner's bed and breakfast where I'm staying. You can follow me there after work and ask her yourself if she's got another room available."

"Thanks." Drake glanced across the room. "I think I can see the wall again."

Grimm nodded. "Going back to my wall."

Moments later, the men were slamming their heavy sledgehammers into yet more plaster.

Drake worked on the next four feet of wall, knocking out sheetrock. He grabbed hold of a portion of the drywall and pulled hard. A large portion fell away, exposing a gap between studs that was three feet wide.

Had there been a door there at one time? He removed the rest of the plaster down to the floor and had to wait for the dust to settle in order to see the beams, much less if anything lay beyond the beams.

As the dust slowly settled, Drake's headlamp beam cut through the remaining particles to a room beyond the wall. It wasn't more than six feet by six feet square and had been carved out of the rock wall of the mountain.

He stepped between the beams into the stone-walled room. Several wooden crates littered the floor, along with a pile of what appeared to be clothing. He crossed to the crates and found them to be full of bottles of some kind of liquid. None of the bottles were labeled.

Drake suspected the bottles were moonshine and that the stash was left over from the Prohibition Era. He turned the beam of his headlamp to the pile of clothes on the floor. The cloth had a floral pattern of faded pink and yellow. Perhaps it had once been a curtain or a woman's dress.

As he neared the pile, he noticed a shoe and something that appeared to be a pole or thick stick lying beside it.

His pulse picked up, his empty belly roiling. He leaned over the pile of clothes and the shoe and froze.

The stick wasn't a stick at all. It was a bone. On the other side of it was another bone just like it.

With the handle of his sledgehammer, he moved the crate beside the pile of cloth and gasped.

On the other side of the crate, lying against the cold stone floor, lay a skull covered in a dry mummified layer of skin with a few long, thin strands of hair clinging to it in scattered patches.

"Parker," Drake called out.

When the hammering continued, Drake cleared his throat and yelled. "Parker!"

All hammering ceased.

"That you, Drake?" Parker answered.

With his gaze on what he now had determined was a complete skeleton covered in a woman's dress, Drake said, "You need to come see this."

ABOUT THE AUTHOR

ELLE JAMES also writing as MYLA JACKSON is a *New York Times* and *USA Today* Bestselling author of books including cowboys, intrigues and paranormal adventures that keep her readers on the edges of their seats. When she's not at her computer, she's traveling, snow skiing, boating, or riding her ATV, dreaming up new stories. Learn more about Elle James at www.ellejames.com

Website | Facebook | Twitter | GoodReads | Newsletter | BookBub | Amazon

Or visit her alter ego Myla Jackson at mylajackson.com
Website | Facebook | Twitter | Newsletter

Follow Me!
www.ellejames.com
ellejamesauthor@gmail.com

ALSO BY ELLE JAMES

Shadow Assassin

Delta Force Strong

Ivy's Delta (Delta Force 3 Crossover)

Breaking Silence (#1)

Breaking Rules (#2)

Breaking Away (#3)

Breaking Free (#4)

Breaking Hearts (#5)

Breaking Ties (#6)

Breaking Point (#7)

Breaking Dawn (#8)

Breaking Promises (#9)

Brotherhood Protectors Yellowstone

Saving Kyla (#1)

Saving Chelsea (#2)

Saving Amanda (#3)

Saving Liliana (#4)

Saving Breely (#5)

Saving Savvie (#6)

Ranger Creed (#14)

Delta Force Rescue (#15)

Dog Days of Christmas (#16)

Montana Rescue (#17)

Montana Ranger Returns (#18)

Hot SEAL Salty Dog (SEALs in Paradise)

Hot SEAL, Hawaiian Nights (SEALs in Paradise)

Hot SEAL Bachelor Party (SEALs in Paradise)

Hot SEAL, Independence Day (SEALs in Paradise)

Brotherhood Protectors Vol 1

Brotherhood Protectors Vol 2

Brotherhood Protectors Vol 3

Brotherhood Protectors Vol 4

Brotherhood Protectors Vol 5

Brotherhood Protectors Vol 6

Iron Horse Legacy

Soldier's Duty (#1)

Ranger's Baby (#2)

Marine's Promise (#3)

SEAL's Vow (#4)

Warrior's Resolve (#5)

Drake (#6)

Grimm (#7)

Murdock (#8)

Tactical Force (#5)

Disruptive Force (#6)

Mission: Six

One Intrepid SEAL

Two Dauntless Hearts

Three Courageous Words

Four Relentless Days

Five Ways to Surrender

Six Minutes to Midnight

Hearts & Heroes Series

Wyatt's War (#1)

Mack's Witness (#2)

Ronin's Return (#3)

Sam's Surrender (#4)

Take No Prisoners Series

SEAL's Honor (#1)

SEAL'S Desire (#2)

SEAL's Embrace (#3)

SEAL's Obsession (#4)

SEAL's Proposal (#5)

SEAL's Seduction (#6)

SEAL'S Defiance (#7)

Hot Velocity (#4)

Cajun Magic Mystery Series

Voodoo on the Bayou (#1)

Voodoo for Two (#2)

Deja Voodoo (#3)

Cajun Magic Mysteries Books 1-3

SEAL Of My Own

Navy SEAL Survival

Navy SEAL Captive

Navy SEAL To Die For

Navy SEAL Six Pack

Devil's Shroud Series

Deadly Reckoning (#1)

Deadly Engagement (#2)

Deadly Liaisons (#3)

Deadly Allure (#4)

Deadly Obsession (#5)

Deadly Fall (#6)

Covert Cowboys Inc Series

Triggered (#1)

Taking Aim (#2)

Bodyguard Under Fire (#3)

Cowboy Resurrected (#4)

Navy SEAL Justice (#5)

Navy SEAL Newlywed (#6)

High Country Hideout (#7)

Clandestine Christmas (#8)

Thunder Horse Series

Hostage to Thunder Horse (#1)

Thunder Horse Heritage (#2)

Thunder Horse Redemption (#3)

Christmas at Thunder Horse Ranch (#4)

Demon Series

Hot Demon Nights (#1)

Demon's Embrace (#2)

Tempting the Demon (#3)

Lords of the Underworld

Witch's Initiation (#1)

Witch's Seduction (#2)

The Witch's Desire (#3)

Possessing the Witch (#4)

Stealth Operations Specialists (SOS)

Nick of Time

Alaskan Fantasy

Made in the USA
Las Vegas, NV
19 November 2022

59877247R00144